Jerry th
Volu

D0735837

Part of the Arestana Series

Shawn P. B. Robinson

BrainSwell

BrainSwell Publishing
Ingersoll, Ontario

ISBN 978-1-7751903-7-0

Interior Map by Allan Jensen
Artwork copyright © Shawn Robinson

BrainSwell Publishing
Ingersoll, ON

Dedication and Thanks

To my wonderful wife who has tolerated my sense of humor along with my odd imagination. To my two sons, Liam and Ezra, who grew up hearing these stories.
To all the Squirrels who have understood that I mean them no ill by telling stories about their Arestanian counterparts.
To Hat Squirrel who is clearly a wonderful leader. Hats off to Hat Squirrel.
To Juanita, Hollie, Liam, Ezra and my Mother-In-Law who have helped get these stories out to the unsuspecting public.

Now, for those of you who like allegory or deeper meaning in books, please understand that this book is intended not to have deeper meaning or allegory. Feel free to search for it, but don't be disappointed if you come up with really insightful meanings for characters or experiences or places and at the end of the day… you're just wrong. ☺ Characters/places/etc. do not represent anything else (even in the book). It's a fun book. Everything is fiction in this book.

Preface

These stories have grown out of bedtime stories I used to tell my sons back in the day. I would make the stories up (often as I told them) and have lots of fun listening to them laugh (either at the stories or at me, I'm not sure).

The stories are actually set in the world of Arestana which is a world I created for the Arestana Trilogy. If you enjoy these short stories, let me encourage you to check out Arestana: The Key Quest.

I hope you enjoy the whacky sense of humor contained within these pages. May they be a lot of fun for you to read.

Shawn P. B. Robinson

Books by Shawn P. B. Robinson
Available in Print or ebook

Jerry the Squirrel: Volume I
Jerry the Squirrel: Volume II
Arestana I: The Key Quest
Arestana II: The Defense Quest
Arestana III: The Harry Quest

Coming Soon

Jerry the Squirrel: Volume III   Coming 2019

www.shawnpbrobinson.com

www.amazon.com/author/shawnpbrobinson

www.facebook.com/shawnpbrobinsonauthor/

@shawnpbrobinson

Table of Contents

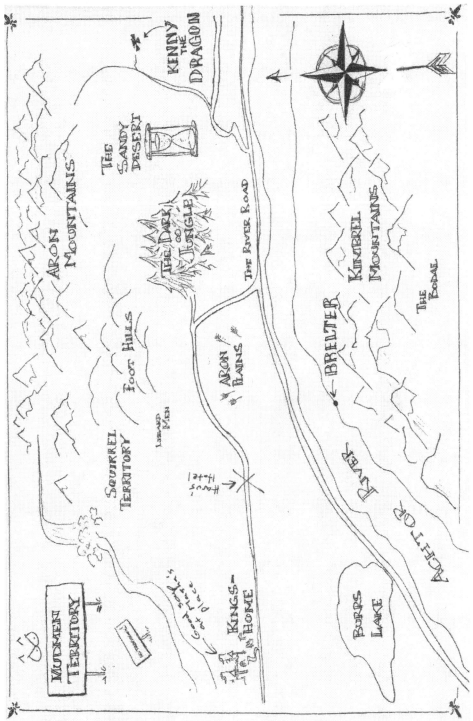

1

Killer Slippers Part I

Jerry was a Squirrel. Jerry was also an inventor... quite a good one, as a matter of fact. He could design and build just about anything. The problem was, Jerry's inventions rarely worked the way he wanted them to work.

Jerry opened his eyes. He stared up at the ceiling for a moment before turning his head and looking around. It was too early to get up, but he was awake. Once he was awake, he just had to get up.

He pulled back the covers on his little Squirrel bed and swung his legs around. He looked down at the floor and groaned to himself. The floor was always so cold in the morning, and he always forgot to leave his slippers by the bed. Looking around the room, Jerry spied them over by his work desk. He did not want to step on the cold floor without his slippers, but the slippers were so far away.

1

He looked at the walls around his room. In his bedroom, there was the bed, a dresser with no clothes in it (Squirrels do not wear clothing) and his work desk where he worked on his inventions. There were two windows in the room showing the cool, beautiful morning outside. He realized he could jump to the dresser, then from there to a window ledge. From there, if he could turn just right, he thought he might be able to swing over to his desk, reach down to the floor and grab his slippers. Then he could put them on before stepping down on the cold, cold floor.

Jerry crawled to the end of his bed and took a look at the distance between the end of his bed and the edge of his dresser. It wasn't too far, but he was afraid of missing, so he threw his pillow down on the floor... just in case. He bent his legs to jump and opened his hands to grab the dresser. He had to put a lot of strength into his jump. It was a long way, and he didn't want to miss.

He readied himself and then leapt with all his might toward the dresser! He knew right away that he had jumped hard enough. He had strong legs. Unfortunately, he realized that with this much power, he had jumped much harder than he needed to.

He slammed nose first into the wall, well above the dresser, and rolled back. He missed the pillow on the way down and landed right on the cold floor. This day was turning out pretty normal. He didn't understand why he couldn't get that jump just right. He had tried it every morning for months!

He stood up. His feet were already cold, and he hopped over to his slippers. Picking them up, he put them on one at a time before heading to the kitchen for some breakfast.

His kitchen was much like his bedroom. It also had a cold floor. He didn't like that, but at least he had his slippers on.

The room had a table with two chairs, one for himself and one for a guest. There was a large barrel beside the table, filled with water for drinking. Beside the barrel was a giant box where he kept the nuts for everyday eating. The nuts he had collected for winter were down below in his basement. He walked to the nut box and grabbed a couple of nuts.

Something was on his mind, but he couldn't figure it out. There was something he had to do. He had to invent. But what? What should he invent today?

He looked down at his cold floor. He could come up with some way of heating the floor, but he was sure that the rest of the village would not be happy. Chances were, whatever he invented to heat his floor would burn half the village down.

He could invent slippers that could keep his feet warm, but that wasn't the problem. The problem was that his slippers were always far away from his bed in the morning.

He continued to think through his problem as he chewed a few more nuts in his mouth and took a big drink from the water barrel.

Maybe he could solve the slipper problem. His floor was cold, but what if he always had warm slippers nearby? He could invent a machine that made new slippers for him every morning. He thought about that for a moment before giving up on the idea. He realized that idea was ridiculous. If he tried to make new slippers every morning, where would he get enough warm fuzzy material?

Finally, the perfect idea hit him! Maybe... just maybe he could create slippers that would come to his bed when he called!

Jerry ran back into his bedroom and sat down at his desk. He grabbed all the papers and books and drawings on his desk and threw them aside. He grabbed a large piece of paper, spread it out before himself and went to work on the designs for his new invention.

After about an hour, he sat back and looked at his design. He had designed the ultimate slippers. They weren't built yet, but the plans were all laid out on paper. The slippers would be warm and fuzzy and would look great on him in the morning. They would also have a microphone built into them to receive commands from him. He could speak commands such as, "Come here!" and "Stop chewing on the dog!" to control the slippers. He had also designed little wheels on the bottom so the slippers could move. They could drive forward and backward. They could turn left and right. He had even given them treads, so they had some traction in case the floor was slippery.

He set to work on building his slipper invention. He found designing a new invention was always the easy part.

Building the new gadget, on the other hand, was usually much harder. He worked all morning, right through the afternoon and into the evening before stopping for a break.

Around supper time, he stopped for a moment to go into the kitchen and grab some nuts and water before he quickly returned to his desk. The slippers were nearly built. He only needed to install the wheels and program the microphone to receive his commands. He set to work again, and within a couple more hours he was done. He stepped back and stared at his creation.

They were red slippers with white fuzzy material on the inside and around the top. They were well padded, so they would be comfortable. The wheels on the bottom were solid and made of a black rubber material. On the top was a small microphone. It could hardly be seen, but it would work just fine.

Jerry was exhausted. Every invention was so much work, and he couldn't wait to try out the slippers. He was just about to see if they would work, but he realized it wouldn't do to try them out that night. The time to try them out was in the morning when the floor was cold.

He carefully set the slippers down on the floor by his desk, a long way away from his bed. He prepared himself to go to bed by brushing and flossing all twenty of his teeth and combing his hair. His hair always stuck up in strange places. He liked that. He always felt bad for those poor Squirrels who had smooth, well-combed hair. Poor things.

After a long day of inventing, he was so tired. He crawled into bed and was sound asleep in minutes!

He woke up the next morning and stared at the ceiling. It was a cool morning, and he was already feeling a little chilly.

Jerry sat up and swung his legs over the side of the bed. He looked down at the floor and groaned. The floor was always so cold in the mornings. He looked around his room, and his eyes landed on his slippers. They were all the way over by his desk. He was about to jump over to his dresser when he remembered that he had invented Automatic Slippers! He didn't need to go anywhere! They would come to him.

He looked back at the slippers on the floor by his desk and smiled. He opened his mouth and hollered out, "Slippers! Come here!"

He was thrilled to see the slippers instantly respond by turning toward him and rolling smoothly to the bed. As they arrived at the foot of the bed, they turned around neatly, so Jerry was able to easily slide his feet into each of the slippers. They were warm and cozy. He smiled to himself, thinking he might never again have to feel the cold floor on his poor toes in the morning. He had solved his cold floor problem!

He stood up and hollered out his next command, "Slippers, take me to the kitchen!"

Nothing happened at first. He was worried he would have to go back to the drawing board. Maybe the mic wasn't working properly, or the command was too much for the slippers to understand. He breathed a sigh of relief when they finally started to move. They turned and began to roll toward the kitchen.

As he rolled into the kitchen, he hollered out, "Slippers, take me to my food!"

This time, there was no pause. The slippers rolled him right to the food, and he was able to get a drink from the barrel and grab a few nuts to eat to start out his morning! Jerry was thrilled! His invention was turning out just as he had hoped.

He thought he would try something a little more difficult. "Slippers, take me for a walk around the neighborhood!"

He didn't think this would work, but he wanted to try it. He wanted to see what the slippers could do.

He cheered out loud the instant his slippers made for the door. As soon as he was within reach of the door, he stretched out his hand to grab the door handle.

The slippers, however, had another plan. He was shocked to find that the slipper on his right foot, with his right foot still in it, leapt into the air, kicked his hand out of the way and grabbed the doorknob. Within seconds, the door was open, and Jerry was rolling out the door, rubbing his hand in pain.

He wasn't too pleased with the kick but was happy to know that the slippers could figure out how to open doors on their own. This would mean if they were ever stuck in a closet, they could get themselves out so they could come to him and warm his feet.

He rolled forward just a little bit before the same slipper, the one on his right foot, shot out behind him. It grabbed the door handle and pulled the door shut behind him. He nearly fell over on his face when it happened, but just managed to keep himself upright. It did, however, hurt a lot. His leg wasn't used to twisting like that.

As he rolled around the neighborhood, the other Squirrels stared at him in shock. His feet and legs weren't moving, but he was rolling along. No one was able to figure out how he was moving.

None of the other Squirrels like to invent. Jerry was a bit of an odd one that way. They put up with him because they liked some of his inventions, but they just didn't understand the whole "inventing thing."

Jerry thought he would give his neighbors a bit of a show. It was fun to let them watch as he slowly rolled around the neighborhood, but maybe if he were going a bit faster, it would be better.

"Slippers, go faster!" Jerry yelled.

Instantly he picked up speed. He hadn't told the slippers how fast they should go so he worried they would move too fast, but instead, they seemed to know exactly how fast he wanted to go!

He zoomed around the neighborhood as the other Squirrels watched in fascination. Many of them waved, and the Squirrel children squeaked with joy. He looked up ahead and saw the house belonging to Mary the Squirrel. She had a nice little flower garden out front which stood up a little higher than everyone else's flower garden. He often thought that it looked just like a ramp.

He hollered out, "Slippers, jump Mary's garden ramp!"

The slippers turned and picked up speed. Jerry bent his knees and leaned forward. This was going to be good. He was sure he would get some good air on this one.

Mary seemed to sense what Jerry was up to and came screaming out of her house. "NO!" she yelled. "Not my petunias!"

She was too slow. She couldn't make it to the garden in time. Jerry hit the edge of the garden moving so fast the rest of the world was a blur. He didn't think the slippers could go this fast, but it was happening. He raced up the side of the garden and off the top, taking most of Mary's flowers with him. He looked down and realized he was soaring above all the Squirrel houses. This... was... awesome!

He then realized the problem. It wasn't the launch that was dangerous, it was the landing. He had not figured out ahead of time how to land without hurting himself. He stopped yelling out in joy and began to yell out in terror. The Squirrels below couldn't tell the difference, and all of them, aside from Mary, cheered him on.

He came down and landed hard on the slippers, but they survived the landing. He wasn't hurt, but the slippers were now making funny noises. He hoped he hadn't damaged them.

"Slippers, stop!" he yelled as hundreds of Squirrels came up to him. They all had looks of amazement on their faces, and each one began to beg Jerry to make them a pair as well.

He told them a price of how much each would cost and started taking orders. In the end, over one hundred Squirrels wanted a pair!

When he had all the orders, he yelled out, "Slippers, take me home!"

His slippers began to move, but he was sure he heard them make a funny noise. It sounded almost like the slippers were upset.

To be continued…

2

Killer Slippers Part II

The next morning Jerry woke up excited about his day's plans. He knew his slippers were the best slippers in the world. There was no need to jump on his dresser, and he didn't have to step on the cold floor. Instead, he jumped out of bed and into the air, without his slippers on his feet. While in the air, he hollered out, "Slippers, warm my feet!"

Just before he landed on the ground, he felt the familiar warmth of his cozy footwear slide themselves neatly onto his feet. He landed in comfort, and within moments he was in the kitchen, having a nice breakfast of nuts he'd collected in days gone by.

This was going to be a good day! He would finish his breakfast, head to his desk and set to work on the hundreds of orders of slippers. He knew he could move fast on them. Building the first set took most of the day, but now that he knew how to build slippers, he could produce maybe ten or fifteen a day. This was going to be great.

BANG, BANG, BANG!

Jerry turned to the door. Who could be at his door this early in the morning? He commanded his slippers to take him to the door and as he arrived, one of his slippers, foot inside, kicked up, grabbed the door handle and swung the door open. Unfortunately for Jerry, the slipper held the door handle, and he had to stand there with his legs stretched out like he was doing the splits. He tried to make it look natural.

Standing outside his house was just about every Squirrel in Erry-ville. They all looked happy and excited. Jerry was relieved to see that. Typically when the Squirrels showed up at his house, it meant they were really upset with him. Today, however, they seemed pleased.

"May I help you?" Jerry asked the crowd.

Terry the Squirrel stepped forward, along with Larry. They looked at Jerry a little funny as if noticing for the first time that he was doing the splits. Terry spoke first. "We, um… are wondering if our slippers are ready."

"Yah," Larry piped in. "I have cold toes. I have poor circulation. I need something to keep them warm."

Everyone began to holler out, "Where are our slippers?" and "Are they ready yet?"

Jerry raised his hands, while still doing the splits with the one foot holding the door open. "Squirrels of Erry-Ville, hear me!" Jerry thought that sounded good. "I, Jerry the first, would like to…"

Mary hollered out from the crowd and cut him off. "Wait! Your dad and grandpa were both named Jerry. I think your great-grandpa was named Jerry too! Aren't you Jerry the fourth?"

Jerry felt he was losing control of the conversation. He decided to get to the point. "The slippers aren't ready yet! I should have some of them finished by tomorrow."

With that, the slipper slammed the door closed and returned to the floor. He was sweating. The Squirrels outside looked angry that their slippers weren't ready. He closed his eyes. He felt the stress of having to get all those orders finished.

He could feel a little bit of sweat build on his forehead and reached up to wipe away the sweat. As his hand arrived at his forehead, it was pushed aside. He opened up his eyes to see one of his slippers with his left foot inside. It was there, with his leg stretched up. It wiped his forehead for him.

"Um, thanks, but I think I can wipe my own forehead," he said to the slippers.

The slipper pulled back and turned toward his face. It did not look happy. He felt it was not fair that a slipper should be able to look unhappy. He also felt it was not fair that the other slipper decided it also wanted to look him in the eye with an angry look. The second slipper shot up and looked him directly in the eye, beside the first slipper.

For a second, he hung suspended in mid-air, with both feet stuck in a slipper, staring him in the eyes. It wasn't long, however, before he came crashing down. He was about to tell them off for making him fall when he heard one of the slippers growl. He didn't like where this was going.

The slippers then dropped to the floor and, without waiting for him to stand up first, began to roll in the direction of his desk, dragging him behind. Within moments, they had seated him in his chair. Both slippers sat on the desk, feet still inside, watching him.

It made him nervous to be watched by slippers, but he decided to ignore the weirdness of it all and set to work. He loved building new inventions. This was one of his favorite parts of his job. As he built, he quickly lost track of time and forgot that his slippers were staring at him, watching his every move.

After many hours, he leaned back in his chair and stared at the pile of slippers he had built. They were all different styles and sizes. They looked good.

He stretched and went back to work and kept at it until the sun set. It had taken him all day, but he finished twenty sets of slippers. This was far more than he had expected to make in one day. He was pleased with a job well done.

Jerry took the time to quickly test each one to make sure each pair worked properly before turning back to his bed. He was tired and ready for a good night's sleep. He put his head down on the pillow and was out in seconds. He slept well but had strange dreams. He dreamed his slippers were angry with him, and they were telling him to work harder and faster. He didn't like it when his own inventions yelled at him. He also didn't like the idea of slippers that could speak. He didn't feel that was appropriate for slippers.

Nevertheless, Jerry woke up feeling refreshed. He pulled back the covers and swung his feet around. He was about to call out for his slippers when he gasped. He looked around the room, shocked to see what had happened. Sometime in the night, hundreds of slippers had been made. He knew he hadn't made them. There was no way he could have built so many in such a short amount of time!

He looked at his desk and saw the answer. His slippers sat there, on the desk. They were hard at work building more slippers. He was impressed, although a little disturbed.

"Slippers, come here!" he hollered.

The slippers stopped what they were doing and looked over at him. At the same moment, all the slippers in the room turned to him. He had a moment, just a moment, to cry out in fear as he realized what he had done. He had not told them which pair of slippers he had wanted to come to him.

Hundreds of slippers at that moment charged him, all hoping to be the slippers which had the privilege of warming his feet that particular morning. He crawled farther back on his bed as they came after him.

"No! No! Not all of you! I can't wear all of you!"

They didn't stop. They just kept coming. They arrived at his feet, all at the same time. Each pair began to battle for his feet. Most of the slippers felt the best way to claim a foot was to pull on a toe. Each of his five toes on each foot felt like they were being pulled in a different direction. His feet did not enjoy the experience.

"Oooooowww!!!" Jerry screamed. He remembered that he had to command them a certain way. "Slippers, stop!" The slippers stopped what they were doing, but many still had a grip on one of his toes. "Slippers, let go of my toes and back away!"

They backed away, and he looked down at his feet. He was shocked. He didn't think toes could bend that way. Clearly, he was wrong.

"Slippers! My slippers! The slippers that I made the other day and wore outside yesterday! Come here!"

One of the pairs of slippers came forward. He picked them up and held them for all to see. "Slippers! This pair of slippers in my hand will be called, 'My Slippers.' So when I call, 'My Slippers,' the rest of you just ignore it, okay?"

They all nodded in agreement. "My Slippers! Fix my toes, and then get on my feet!"

He didn't think his toes could hurt more than they had when they were being pulled in ten different directions, but he was wrong about that as well. He yelled out in pain, but in no time his feet were back to normal and wearing his slippers.

He stepped down on the floor. This was not turning out quite the way he thought it would. His thoughts were interrupted by a loud knock on his front door.

"My Slippers, take me to the door." As he rolled to the door, he remembered he didn't want to do the splits again. He was about to holler out a command to stop the slippers from grabbing the handle, but he was too late. The door swung open with his slipper holding the handle and his foot still in the slipper. He was doing the splits again and not happy about it.

Outside Jerry's house, there was once again a large crowd of Squirrels assembled. Terry stepped forward as though he was the spokesperson for the town. "We have come for our slippers, Jerry. If you could stop doing the splits and get them for us, we would all appreciate it."

"They are ready!" Jerry said, quite happy that his slippers could be enjoyed by so many Squirrels. That'll be ten nuts a pair."

The Squirrels pulled out bags of various kinds of nuts. This would save Jerry having to collect as much next harvest time.

They each paid and Jerry began to hand out the slippers. The Squirrels immediately put them on. Jerry could hear them command their new slippers to take them various places around the village.

When he was all done handing out slippers, he said, "My Slippers, let's go for a slow trip around the village!"

His slippers began to roll out the door. One of them, at the last moment, swung up with his foot attached and grabbed the door. It pulled the door closed behind him. On the way back, the slipper swung over and kicked him in the butt. It then landed on the ground. He looked at it and yelled, "Why did you do that?" Jerry was sure the slipper shrugged back at him as if to say, "Dunno. But I might do it again."

Jerry decided to ignore it. He looked around and watched in amazement as Squirrels all through the village wore their slippers. No one had to walk anywhere anymore. The slippers just rolled them where they wanted to go. Some Squirrels wandered up and down the streets. Others worked in their gardens. Others rolled through trees, collecting nuts for the winter. Everyone seemed happy. Everyone was at peace.

He continued to roll around the village. Everyone was not only happy, but they seemed pleased with Jerry as well. This didn't happen often, and Jerry was glad. Some of the Squirrels invited him in for a cup of tea. Others invited him over for BBQ nuts on the weekend. Even Hat Squirrel, when he saw Jerry, tipped his hat in Jerry's direction. Life was good.

After a busy day of smiling and chatting with Squirrels, Jerry turned back toward home. What a day! He felt like he was finally starting to fit in with his village.

As he approached the door, he stopped and took one last look around before settling in for the night. Many Squirrels were still outside, enjoying an evening roll down the lane. This was a good day.

"Have a good night, my friends!" Jerry called out to the village. Everyone smiled back at him and waved.

He turned toward his door with the entire village watching. Before he could stop it, one of the slippers shot up and grabbed the door handle. This was bad enough as everyone watched, but what made it worse was that the other slipper decided to push the door open. He landed flat on his back and was dragged inside while everyone watched.

The slippers closed and locked the door, then dragged Jerry to bed. They tucked him in a little too tight for his comfort before rolling back to their spot by the desk.

Jerry quickly fell asleep. He was happy. As he lay there, sleeping peacefully, he was entirely unaware of what was about to happen. This happy day of slippers would be the only happy day the village would have with their slippers.

To be continued...

Killer Slippers Part III

Jerry woke up smiling. What a great couple of days! Everyone had been so happy with their slippers. It was still early in the morning, but he could already hear the sounds of many Squirrels outside. There was a lot of noise. He looked forward to joining them.

"Slippers, come here!" he hollered. Within seconds, he was standing in his room, slippers on his feet. His toes were warm and cozy, and he was content.

"Slippers, take me to my food and water in the kitchen!"

He rolled out into the kitchen toward the food as he continued to listen to the noise of many Squirrels outside. They sounded like they were having so much fun. The screams and yells of many Squirrels in the village was the sound he lived for.

He grabbed some nuts and munched on them for a little bit, thinking about the joy his invention had brought to Erry-Ville. He wondered if Hat Squirrel would reward him for having such an impact on his community. This was going to be a good day.

He took a drink of water and continued to listen to the sound of the Squirrels outside. He started to be able to pick out some of the words. One of the words he picked out was, "Nooooo!!!" He thought that was odd. Perhaps some of the Squirrels were trying to jump Mary's Garden ramp as he had the other day. Mary probably wasn't too happy about that. He smiled to himself.

He continued to munch on more nuts. He needed to keep up his strength. Perhaps Squirrels would come from other villages today. Word of his great invention would likely travel throughout Arestana. Soon everyone would want a pair of his slippers. He ate more nuts. He would need energy to make that many slippers!

He listened some more to the sounds coming in from outside. He could hear many cries and screams of Squirrels and the sound of yells mixed with fear and pain.

He wasn't sure why they would sound so upset while wearing such wonderful slippers, but perhaps they had their reasons. Another voice drifted in. This one screamed, "Heeeeeeeelp!" He thought that was quite odd. Normally Squirrels didn't yell out the word, "Help" when they were having fun. It was a word most Squirrels knew not to overuse. There was the story, of course, of the Squirrel Who Cried Hawk. No one wanted to be that Squirrel.

He heard the scream for help again, along with many other Squirrels calling for help. Perhaps there was something else going on, and he should roll outside to see if he could offer assistance.

He finished up his breakfast, wiped his chin and said, "Slippers, take me outside."

He rolled over to the door. When he arrived at the door, the slipper on his right foot leapt up, grabbed the door handle and swung it open. The other slipper rolled out while the slipper on his right foot pulled the door closed behind him. He didn't enjoy the feeling of pain as his legs stretched and twisted every which way, but he knew he'd get used to it eventually. Or maybe he would fix the problem with the slippers. He wasn't sure which would happen first.

He took a deep breath and looked around. What he saw caused the hair on the back of his neck to stand up.

Hundreds of Squirrels were racing around the village and up and down the trunks of trees. Their slippers were going nuts! Not the food kind of nuts, but the other kind. They were out of control!

Every Squirrel wearing slippers was being dragged all over the place. Squirrels were crying out in fear and yelling for help, but no one could help them because everyone else was wearing slippers and being dragged around as well! Everyone looked terrified. The damage which had already taken place in the village was unbelievable! Every house appeared to have at least one broken window, and the door on each and every house had a Squirrel shaped hole smashed through it. Jerry's own home appeared to be the only one untouched.

The slippers had gone haywire.

Some of the Squirrels, as they were being dragged up and down trees and around the village, noticed Jerry standing there. They cried out for help, "Jerry! Help us! The slippers are going nuts! We don't mean the food kind of nuts. It would be okay if they were going that kind of nuts! No, they are not going that kind of nuts. They are going the other kind of nuts! We don't like the kind of nuts they are going! Help us!"

Jerry wasn't sure what to do. He had no idea how to stop all the slippers. They wouldn't listen to him, would they? He thought he'd try. "Slippers! All you slippers belonging to everyone else! Stop!"

Instantly, all the slippers stopped wherever they were. Some had been in the process of rolling up a tree and hung there, with their Squirrels hanging below them. Others were in the middle of a jump over Mary's garden. They somehow managed to stop mid-air! They all turned and looked right at Jerry. He thought maybe they were going to put an end to their destruction and go back to normal. He hoped that would be what they would do. Instead, they all started rolling toward him.

He hoped they were coming back so he could fix them, but when the slippers arrived close, with the Squirrels still in them, each one stopped and looked at him. One by one, they all began to bend down their toes as if they were bowing to him.

Jerry thought maybe the slippers all thought he was their king since he had made them. That made him feel good. They liked him. He liked being liked.

As he watched them, however, he realized they were not bowing to him. They were bowing to his own slippers. He looked down in fear to see his slippers lifting up the toes and waving back at the slippers as they bowed.

"Slippers! What's going on?" Jerry hollered out.

The slippers turned up toward him. He wasn't sure how, but they appeared to be smiling at him. He wasn't sure he liked the way this was going.

He heard some grunts coming from the Squirrels and looked back up again. Each of the slippers worn by the other Squirrels were now jumping up in the air as if they were making kicking movements. Each slipper kick dragged the leg of the Squirrel it was attached to up in the air. Jerry stared with horror, realizing that each of the kicks were meant for him.

"Slippers! No! Bad slippers! Stop this, Slippers!" he yelled out. He looked down at his own slippers to see the smile grow even bigger.

He felt the movement. It was slight, at first, but it was there. His slippers were rolling just a little bit, but not forward, backward or even sideways. They were turning Jerry around, so he was facing the other way.

"What? Slippers, what are you doing? Stop this! Slippers! Stop turning me around!"

He looked back over his shoulders to see the rest of the Squirrels being dragged toward him by their slippers.

His own slippers had betrayed him. They had turned him around so he would be ready for a good butt-kicking.

Each of the slippers took their turns, kicking and making an odd sound like a giggle. One by one, each Squirrel was dragged forward by their slippers and then the slippers, both feet, right and left, each took their turn giving Jerry a huge kick. At first, he yelled at his slippers to stop, then he tried to pull his feet out of the slippers. There was no hope. He was stuck there for the entire butt-kicking experience.

The Squirrels themselves were all very upset by this. They didn't enjoy kicking Jerry, and they each apologized in turn. Each Squirrel apologized... aside from Mary. She mumbled something about her garden not being a ramp and how Jerry deserved this.

When they were done, he was sore. He was also very unhappy.

He looked down at his slippers and tried to think of a way to put a stop to this madness. His slippers were not obeying him anymore, and neither were anyone else's. They had to be stopped. There had to be a way. He had an idea. Maybe if he could turn the slippers against one another.

"Slippers," he whispered, bending down so he could get close and speak privately to his own slippers. Some of the slippers took that as an invitation to start kicking again, but he ignored it.

He continued to whisper. "Slippers, did you see what that other pair of slippers did a moment ago? Do you think that pair of slippers wants to be king instead of you?"

Jerry's slippers turned back quickly toward the rest of his slippers. This had the unfortunate effect of putting Jerry's face in the same spot where his butt had been a few minutes ago. It took a few kicks before the slippers appeared to realize they weren't connecting with his butt anymore.

His own slippers began to eye each of the other slippers, one by one. Each of the slippers bowed down again to him, but Terry's slippers didn't notice Jerry's slippers were looking his way. That pair didn't bow, and it was all Jerry's slippers needed.

They charged toward Terry and his slippers. Seeing Jerry come at him full speed, Terry cried out in fear. Jerry wasn't sure how this would turn out but hoped it would help the situation. When he reached Terry, Jerry and Terry collided in a pile of fur and pain.

Terry cried out in fear again, "Help! Your slippers are trying to eat my feet!"

Jerry looked at his feet and, sure enough, his slippers were swallowing Terry's feet. Well, not his feet, exactly, but Terry's slippers. In a few seconds, Terry's slippers had been completely eaten by Jerry's slippers. Terry was free. Success! It was working.

Jerry looked again at his slippers and could see that they were mad. He could see as well that the other slippers were all mad. No slippers wanted to be eaten by another pair of slippers. That was just weird. And it seemed wrong.

It also seemed to be too much for the rest of the slippers, and now none of the slippers were bowing to

Jerry's slippers. They looked quite upset and started to advance on Jerry's feet.

As they approached, one of the slippers rolled across the toes of another pair of slippers and immediately those two pairs of slippers started to fight each other. In seconds, hundreds of slippers were attacking one another. Some were trying to eat other slippers. Some were kicking the owners of slippers. Some were simply stinking as footwear often does. It was, once again, nuts.

Squirrels began to yell out in fear again, but each time a battle between two pairs of Squirrels was finished, one more Squirrel ran free. Slowly, one by one, each of the Squirrels became slipper-less. In the end, it was just Mary and Jerry left wearing slippers. The last of the freed Squirrels had made it back to their homes.

The streets were empty. Jerry and Mary stood face to face, only a nut's throw away from one another.

Mary was busy trying to tell her slippers to stop. She looked up at Jerry and frowned. "I blame you for all of this, Jerry!"

Jerry was shocked! Sure, he had built the slippers. Sure, he had sold them to everyone. Sure it was his design and the slippers were the way they were because of the design, but that didn't mean it was his fault, did it?

Jerry looked down at his slippers and whispered, "Slippers. There's only one other pair left. Do you think those slippers are your friends or your enemies?"

His slippers looked at the other pair of slippers, and both pairs growled at one another. They charged so quickly that Jerry and Mary fell back and landed on the ground. They were being dragged toward one another at a super-fast speed!

When they had just about reached one another, both pairs leapt into the air and met each other for battle. Jerry didn't like the way his toes felt as his and Mary's feet crashed into one another. It was kind of painful.

They landed on the ground again, and the battle continued. Neither pair of slippers was ready to give up. They kept fighting, dragging Jerry and Mary everywhere they went.

Jerry thought it was time to help out matters a little bit. "Slippers, watch out! The only way to stop this is to eat the other pair!"

Jerry's slippers grabbed hold of Mary's slippers and started to eat them. As he watched, he wondered how his slippers had managed to eat so many other slippers and still be the same size.

When the meal was finished, Mary stood up. She looked at Jerry as he sat on the ground. "I'm still upset at you for using my flower garden as a ramp." With that, she turned and stormed off.

The crisis was over. All the slippers were gone. All the slippers, of course, except Jerry's.

He wasn't sure what to do about them. He liked the slipper, but they were a little on the evil side of things. Jerry didn't like the evil part. As he sat on the ground, he stared down at the slippers. They stared back at him. He stared some more at them. They continued to stare at him. He knew what had to be done. He could not have slippers around that could cause so much damage. He had to end this.

"Slippers! All the other pairs of slippers are gone, but do you think the other slipper on my other foot really likes you? Or do you think he's just like the other slippers?"

Both of his slippers quickly turned to face each other. Since they were still on Jerry's feet, this hurt—a lot. They growled at one another before attacking. They kicked and bit each other, neither one willing to give in. Jerry realized it must have looked pretty funny to anyone else who could see. His two feet were kicking and attacking each other.

It took a while, but finally, the one slipper gobbled up the other.

He looked down at the final remaining slipper, and it looked pleased with itself. It had risen to the top! It was undefeated! It was the best! It was King of the Slippers!

"Slipper!" Jerry yelled. It looked up at him, twisting his foot upwards. "Slipper! There's a problem! You know there's a problem, right?"

The slipper looked back at Jerry and nodded its... head? Toe area?

"Slipper! You know that slippers are meant to come in pairs. I'm going to have to put you in the closet until I build another slipper for my other foot. You understand, right?"

The slipper nodded its toe area again. It slowly slid off Jerry's foot and onto the ground. Jerry quickly picked it up and walked back to his house.

The other Squirrels by this time had realized the slipper-tastrophy was over and began to come out of their houses. It was time to rebuild. It was time to fix all the houses and the roads which had been damaged by the slippers. It was time to go back to normal.

Cold feet no longer seemed to be a big problem for anyone.

Nut Harvester

Jerry was a Squirrel. Jerry was also an inventor... quite a good one, as a matter of fact. He could design and build just about anything. The problem was, Jerry's inventions rarely worked the way he wanted them to work.

Jerry stepped out of his house and took a deep breath. He loved the smell of the fall air. It was mid-September, and the harvest was in full swing. Squirrels were working hard to get all the food they needed to carry them through the winter, the spring and through to the next harvest. The Squirrels of Erry-ville were jumping from branch to branch, collecting nuts in their mouths. When their mouths were full, they would return to their houses to store the nuts. This was what Squirrels were all about. Everyone was happy this time of year.

Everyone, of course, except Barrie. Every fall, right at nut harvest time, Barrie would get a terrible head cold. He would get all stuffed up, his nose would run, and he would get all clingy. He just felt horrible and wanted Squirrels all around him to help make him feel better. That would be fine if all the Squirrels weren't busy collecting nuts, but they were.

To add to all this, Barrie would be so sick, he couldn't climb trees very well. That meant everyone else in the village had to help him with his own harvest.

"My dose is all 'tuffed up," Barrie said to Jerry as he stood in front of his house.

"What?" Jerry said, turning around to see Barrie only a few steps away. He hadn't seen Barrie walk up to him. He had been too focused on the beautiful fall weather to notice the other Squirrel.

"My dose. My dose is all 'tuffed up. I can't breathe," Barrie said, looking very sad.

"Oh, I'm sorry to hear that, Barrie. Ummm... I'd love to hang out, but I have a lot of work to do," Jerry said. He was feeling bad about not being able to spend the time with Barrie, but he had to harvest nuts. Everyone did or else they would starve. Only Barrie seemed able to avoid it every year, but only because of his cold.

The cold made Barrie slow and a little unsteady. If he climbed high up in the tree while he was sick, he would always slip and fall. Since his nose was so full of snot, the landing was never a pretty sight. As a matter of fact, it was so disgusting that the other Squirrels were willing to do the work of collecting a little extra for Barrie so the snot-making Squirrel wouldn't have to climb and splat.

"Cad you get me some duts too? I deed some duts to eat for the widter, so I don't starve to dead," Barrie said.

"Um, yah," Jerry replied. "Of course I'll get a little extra for you. Everyone always grabs a little extra for you, Barrie. Don't worry, we'll take care of you. We always do. Every year."

Jerry said his good-bye and started up the side of a nearby tree. He had been working on collecting from that tree the day before and knew there were some more nuts up there somewhere. It was a big job collecting enough nuts every year. Although he enjoyed it, it was a lot of work.

Whenever he thought of work, his mind started to spin with ideas for inventions. He wondered if there was an easier way to collect nuts. He stopped on a branch and looked down at poor Barrie. He thought about the nuts up in the trees. Every nut had to be found, pulled off the branch and taken back to a house for storage. It would take them weeks every single year. There had to be a better way!

He liked to think of problems like this. The more he thought about these kinds of problems, the more ideas would pop into his head. He thought about creating a machine that could grow the nuts in his house, but he wasn't sure that would work. He also thought he could design a special kind of tree that could grow large enough nuts that two or three would be all the food they would need for an entire year. He stopped to think about that one for a moment, but then realized if one of those nuts broke off and fell to the ground, it could cause terrible damage.

It came to him. He would create a harvester. An automatic harvester could help out the whole village, especially Barrie!

He turned around and raced down the trunk. Barrie saw him coming and started toward him. Jerry knew Barrie would just want to talk about his cold and ask Jerry to collect some nuts for him, but he didn't have the time. When Jerry had an idea for an invention, he had to get to it!

He hollered out, "Can't talk now, Barrie!" and raced on to his house. He slammed the door behind him and locked it tight against interruptions. It was time to focus!

He sat down at his desk and set to work. He worked all morning on the design, and as he worked, he smiled to himself about how easy this invention was. It was coming together without any trouble at all.

By lunchtime, his designs for the machine were ready, and he set to work on putting it together. He had to build most of his inventions in secret. He was a good inventor, and he knew that. The whole village and just about every Squirrel in Arestana knew that he was a good inventor. Unfortunately, sometimes his inventions didn't turn out the way he meant them to.

The mistakes weren't that bad. No one had died or anything, but it wasn't unusual for Squirrels to lose fur, for houses to burn down, for everyone to be left covered in paint or for entire nations to have to leave their lands and settle somewhere else. Because of this, he usually had to keep his work private until it was completed.

The Nut Harvester he was creating was quite large. Back behind his bedroom, he had a larger workroom with a big door leading out behind his house. He also had a lot of his tools back there, so any large inventions were assembled in that location. This invention was going to be huge. He would need the big door to get it outside.

He began to build and was pleased to see it all come together quickly. It had two large arms, one out each side. The large arms would be for climbing trees. They had sharp claws on the end of each arm to grab hold of the bark, and the gears were strong enough to pull the machine way up to reach the nuts.

Up above the large arms, the machine had two smaller arms for grabbing nuts. These could stretch out quite far and were very fast. At the back was a large basket where the collected nuts could be stored. He figured the basket could hold a hundred and fifty nuts before it had to be emptied.

Below the basket was a small hole which worked as a nut dispenser. The harvester could collect the nuts and then pour them out for Squirrels through that hole. If this harvester worked as fast as he hoped it would, one Nut Harvester could do the harvesting for the entire village!

He worked all afternoon and into the evening. He knew the Squirrels would be so happy when they saw his invention. Maybe even Hat Squirrel, the Squirrel leader, would come over for nut-tea and crackers with nuts in them. He wondered if Hat Squirrel would order Jerry to build one for each Squirrel village throughout Arestana! A new day was dawning for the Squirrels!

Jerry finished up and looked out the window. He could see the sun was just beginning to set. He would have to wait until the next day to show the village his new invention.

He slept soundly that night. He dreamed of Harvesters being built and distributed all across the land. He would name them something really creative... something very exciting! He would call them, "Jerry's Nut Harvester!" He wondered if the name needed a bit more work.

At the crack of dawn, he jumped out of bed and ran into the other room. He had a breakfast of nuts and water before running back to his workshop and throwing open the door.

The door to his workshop was large and always made a loud noise when it opened. He didn't like this because whenever anyone heard the door open, they would come running to see if they needed to stop Jerry from inventing. This time they would find they were too late. He was finished!

Sure enough, Squirrels started running toward his house, calling out for Squirrels everywhere to take cover and to prepare for the worst. They arrived in the hundreds and gathered around. Jerry could see the crowd part, and Hat Squirrel made his way to the front.

Hat Squirrel was the leader of the Squirrels. He had been leader for about a month now. The previous Hat Squirrel had been Mary. She had tripped, and the hat had fallen off her head, and then Larry had picked it up and put it on. Whoever wore the hat was Hat Squirrel and therefore the trusted leader of the Squirrel nations. The Squirrel formerly known as "Larry" was now Hat Squirrel.

"What's going on here? Are you thinking of inventing something again, Jerry? You know we don't like that kind of thing!" Hat Squirrel folded his arms in front of his chest and stared at Jerry with a grumpy look on his face.

"Well, Hat Squirrel, sir, I don't mean to be a bother." Jerry was feeling nervous. He didn't like it when everyone looked at him. He wanted to feel important, but he always preferred to work in the background. He didn't like all the attention. "I'm not about to invent something; I've already finished!"

Everyone gasped in terror. Some crouched down while others rolled into a ball and started to rock on the ground. Many of the Squirrels still standing either began to cry or just stared ahead as if all was lost. They looked like they were ready to accept their fate.

"What?" yelled Hat Squirrel. "Have you endangered everyone in the entire land? Are you telling us that we are doomed?"

"No..." Jerry replied. "That seems a little extreme. It's just a harvester."

"A what?" Hat Squirrel asked. The rest of the Squirrels in the crowd began to murmur. They were afraid of what Jerry had invented, but their curiosity was getting the best of them.

"It's a harvester. It's for harvesting nuts. I made it so that it climbs trees, finds the nuts and picks them for us. It'll then bring them down, and we won't have to spend all the time harvesting nuts." Jerry stepped back, put his hand on the harvester and smiled. He was proud of his invention.

"You mean... we won't have to harvest nuts anymore?" one of the Squirrels asked as he stepped forward.

"Nope, this little baby will do all the work for you!" Jerry replied, tapping the harvester on the back. "Think of the hours of work this will save you each and every fall!"

The Squirrels were a funny bunch. They were hard working and loved their work. They were also really lazy and loved to sit around and do nothing. They could get excited about extra work to do, and they could get excited if the work didn't need to be done. This time, they were excited about not having as much work to do.

"I don't know if this is a good idea," Hat Squirrel said. "Will it also cause all the bees in Arestana to go crazy and sting us repeatedly again?"

"No, Hat Squirrel. I told you I was sorry about that. It was all just a misunderstanding. The bees misunderstood the whole situation and overreacted when they saw the giant bear coming for their hives. This won't affect the bees at all," Jerry explained, looking a little embarrassed.

"Well, I don't see the harm in trying this out, as long as the bees aren't upset by it," Hat Squirrel said. "If it'll allow us to not have to harvest nuts every fall, that sounds like a good idea to me."

Everyone cheered and then looked at Jerry. They were all anxious to see it work.

He turned to the Nut Harvester and flipped the switch to the on position. It started to rumble and turn and twist around. Jerry knew it was just trying to figure out where all the nuts were so it could get started, but everyone else cowered in fear.

Once it had spun around a few times, it picked a tree and rushed up the side. In no time, it was hard at work, and in a matter of minutes, it had come down to the bottom of the tree and dumped a pile of nuts on the ground before rushing back up the tree to collect more.

The entire village of Squirrels stared at the pile of nuts. They couldn't believe how fast the machine had harvested their food for them. At the speed it collected nuts, it would likely have enough for all the Squirrels within a day or two.

Jerry turned to look at Hat Squirrel to see a big smile on his face. "Do you like it, Hat Squirrel?" Jerry asked, feeling very proud of himself.

"I love it, Jerry! I love it so much that I hereby claim it for myself. The Nut Harvester from this day forward shall be called, Hat Squirrel's Nut Harvester. I also claim that I invented it," Hat Squirrel declared.

"What? You can't claim that!" Jerry said.

"Pardon me? I think I just did," Hat Squirrel explained. "It is now all mine."

"Good job on the Nut Harvester!" Mary shouted from somewhere in the back of the crowd. "I didn't think you were an inventor too, but you've clearly proven yourself to be an excellent one."

The other Squirrels chimed in as well to congratulate Hat Squirrel on a good invention. He smiled back proudly and even shed a tear, wiping it away with a look in his eye that said, "Thank you, it was hard work, but worth the effort."

The Harvester came down again and dumped another load of nuts on the ground. It did this again and again and again. Within a short amount of time, there was a huge pile of nuts. Jerry was pretty sure the harvester had collected the same amount in about one hour that it would have taken the entire village to collect in two days. The Nut Harvester was amazing... even if it now belonged to Hat Squirrel.

Hat Squirrel's Nut Harvester continued about its business as the Squirrels set to work transferring all the collected nuts to their homes. Since Barrie was so sick and snotty, no one allowed him near the collected nuts. Instead, they carried all the food he needed to his house.

That night, Jerry went to bed, listening to the sound of the Nut Harvester as it continued searching the trees for more nuts. It worked so well. He was proud of what he had accomplished.

The next morning, Jerry stepped out of his house to see the huge pile of nuts had grown larger. There were so many nuts, he realized it was far more than the entire village could eat in a year, maybe even two years!

As he stared at the pile, his thoughts were interrupted by the sound of Hat Squirrel yelling. "Stop! I command you, stop! You are my Nut Harvester! It's time for you to stop collecting nuts! Stop!"

Jerry watched as the Nut Harvester continued to search the trees. It appeared to be having some trouble finding nuts now, but it still found the occasional one.

"What's wrong," Jerry asked.

"My Nut Harvester, you know, the one I invented?" Hat Squirrel asked.

"Yes, I know that Nut Harvester," Jerry said as he rolled his eyes.

"Well, it won't stop. Do you know how to stop it?" Hat Squirrel asked.

"Did you try turning it off? You can flip the same switch I used to turn it on. Just turn that to the off position," he replied.

Hat Squirrel nodded his head and ran over to the Nut Harvester just as it came down to dump another load onto the huge pile. He grabbed for the switch, but just as he reached for it, he tripped and banged his head right on the side.

The Nut Harvester instantly ground to a halt, and Hat Squirrel stood up. He adjusted his hat and smiled at the Nut Harvester. "It's a good thing I put that shut-off switch right there! That's using my head!" he said.

He laughed quite hard at his little joke. He laughed until all the other Squirrels joined in, and he was satisfied they had found it as funny as he had.

Jerry could not help but groan when he heard the laughing. He turned to walk away but stopped as he heard another noise.

The Nut Harvester started to growl. He turned back to see it shaking a lot. The other Squirrels started to gather around and ask Hat Squirrel what was wrong with his invention.

Suddenly the Nut Harvester started to smoke out the top and jumped up in the air about the height of a Squirrel. It held in the air for a moment before crashing down again on the ground. Everyone watched as the Nut Harvester sat still for another moment, then moved quickly over to the pile of nuts. It climbed up on top of the huge pile and began to fill the basket again.

"Whad going on?" Barrie asked as he walked up. "Does that Dut Harvester know that I have a cold?"

Jerry noticed the little dispensing hole on the bottom of the Nut Harvester was doing something a little odd. A small tube appeared out of the hole and came out just a little bit. Jerry had seen enough inventions go wrong that he knew things were about to get messy. He was just about to turn and run when he heard a sound that made his heart stop.

The sound he heard was, "rat-a-tat-a-tat-a-tat" as the Nut Harvester started to fire nuts out of the tube at any and all Squirrels around. The nuts came fast and hard at any Squirrels unlucky enough to be within sight of the machine.

Mary caught four of them in the belly. Her cheeks were full of nuts at the time of impact, but that didn't last long. Her cheeks emptied out on the ground, and she fell over, groaning in agony.

As soon as Mary went down, any Squirrels still standing ran for cover. When an invention went bad, there was nothing to do but run.

Perry and Terry had just started to run for their lives when the Nut Harvester took aim and hit each of them right on their butts. They both went down with a cry of pain.

Hat Squirrel was next. He screamed out in fear, and the Nut Harvester filled his mouth with about one hundred nuts in about two and a half seconds. It was a terrible sight. As the nuts were fired directly into his mouth, his cheeks stretched out, and his eyes grew large. His cheeks grew larger and larger, and Jerry looked away just before he heard a little "pop."

The worst, though, was Barrie. The Nut Harvester was extra cruel to him. He was trying to run away, but every time he saw another Squirrel, he stopped to tell them about his cold. He wasn't getting very far.

He turned back just for a second toward the Nut Harvester, but it was all the time the Nut Harvester needed. It simply fired two nuts at Barrie, one at each nostril. Its aim was true, and both hit with a little splat and sunk right in.

Everyone stopped and stared. They knew what was about to happen, and they knew they should keep running, but it was something they couldn't turn away from. It would be terrible, and it would be gross, but they just had to watch. Curiosity took over.

Barrie stood there for a moment and tried to get the nuts out. He turned to the left and to the right, hoping someone would come to his aid. No one moved. They were all too afraid. The nuts had clogged his nose, and there was nowhere for the snot to go. The snot could do nothing but build up more and more. It could take hours or even days, but the way that Barrie's nose worked, Jerry suspected it would take only minutes.

The moment came sooner than anyone could have imagined. The pressure in the nose built more and more until it could not hold it any longer.

The explosion wasn't so much of an explosion as a very wet splat. No one was safe, not even those who had taken cover behind a tree or bush or even inside a house. Everyone and everything had a thin layer of gross all over them.

When it was done, everyone looked at Barrie. He stood with a smile on his face.

"Hey, everyone! My nose is clear! I can breathe just fine! I'm all better!"

Cold Homes

Jerry was a Squirrel. Jerry was also an inventor... quite a good one, as a matter of fact. He could design and build just about anything. The problem was, Jerry's inventions rarely worked the way he wanted them to work.

Winter was coming on, and it was getting cold outside.

The days were also getting shorter. The sun was coming up a little later in the morning, and it was going down a little earlier. The air was chilly. There was still no snow, but the leaves had all fallen down, and the trees were bare.

Jerry stepped out his front door. Most Squirrels did not like the cold, but Jerry liked cold even less than the other Squirrels. He had always been a smaller Squirrel. He was naturally skinny. The problem with being a skinny

Squirrel was that extra weight helped to keep a Squirrel warm. He had no extra weight, no matter how much he ate.

Jerry did not like the cold at all!

It was still warm enough to get around, and Jerry had a few more things to take care of as he prepared his home for winter. He had to check his roof one more time to make sure it could handle the weight of the snow and the winter winds. He had to make sure that the shutters on all his windows were closed up tight. He had to make sure his house was well insulated to keep out the wind and cold and everything he didn't like about winter.

Jerry stepped outside his house and shivered. He figured he'd better get moving quickly on his work so he could get back inside where it was warm. He started to work on his roof first. He climbed up on top and checked things over. Everything looked just fine.

He was about to move down to the windows when he stopped and scanned the rest of the village. Most of the Squirrels were outside doing just what Jerry was doing, checking over their houses. Everyone was a little worried. They could tell a storm was coming. The temperature was dropping fast. They all feared the first snow would arrive soon.

He climbed down and checked his windows. His house was two stories with an apartment up top. The apartment was empty, but he was thinking of renting it out to another Squirrel sometime. No one was in there right now, but he knew he had to make sure it was just as sealed up as the rest of his house. He checked each of the windows and the shutters over them were all just fine. It wasn't long before he was heading back into his house to warm up.

After he had closed the door, he walked around the inside of the house to check all the insulation. Arestanian Squirrels insulated their houses with dried leaves. Jerry had packed extra leaves in this year since he had been so cold last year. He hoped it would be enough. After seeing that the house was well insulated, he went and huddled in a corner. It wouldn't be long before the storm hit.

He was right. It wasn't long. He could hear the howling of the wind pick up and feel his house shake a little bit. The door creaked, and he could hear leaves and sticks blowing around outside. This was a bigger storm than he had thought it would be.

The temperature was still dropping. He fluffed up his fur a little bit to help keep himself warm.

Walking over to his bed, he climbed in and wrapped himself up with the blankets. Jerry laid there for what seemed like hours, listening to the shutters creak and shift with the power of the wind.

Jerry was cold. He didn't like being cold. There was, however, one thing that was good about being cold. When Jerry was uncomfortable, his inventing mind started to work.

He knew that he didn't like the cold, but he liked the heat. If he liked the heat, he wondered if he could he make something that could heat his home.

An idea struck him, and he jumped out of bed. He was still wearing the blankets. They didn't add as much warmth as his fur did, but they helped a bit.

He started to work. As he worked, he became more and more excited, and in no time at all, the wind and the cold had faded from his mind. It was still windy and even colder than before, but he didn't care. He was inventing! He worked all day long and late into the night.

The next morning, his design was finished. He hadn't built it yet, but he had his idea all worked out. He had not slept one wink, but he knew it was worth it. In no time at all, his house would be warm.

Jerry got to work on building his invention. He always started with a design. He had it now, and the giant heater would soon be ready. He pulled out all sorts of supplies from his closets and various storage spaces around the house. He worked hard and by noon he had his invention completely built!

He opened his door and was shocked to see the snow was so deep it was blocking the entrance to his house! It was like a wall of snow, going way up past the top of his door! He wasn't sure how he could get out, but he was determined. He grabbed the heater, tucked it under his arm and charged. He hit the snow and bounced back onto the floor. He hadn't even made a dent.

He closed up the door and crawled upstairs through a small vent. He wasn't the biggest Squirrel around and sometimes that helped him get through tight spaces.

Once Jerry was on the second floor, he opened up one of the windows and climbed out. He jumped down onto the heavy snow, and it took his weight just fine. The snow was so hard. It must have fallen a little wet and then when the cold winds came, he figured it had probably frozen solid.

He dragged the equipment out onto the hard snow. No one watched him. They were all inside their homes, trying to stay warm.

Jerry walked until he was outside the village and a little ways from his house. He knew the heater would make a little bit of noise and didn't want to disturb his neighbors. They still hadn't forgiven him for the bear attack last summer. He didn't think he could get away with too many more mistakes.

He found his spot and started to dig. At first, it was hard going, but as he made his way through the hard layer on top, it started to get a little easier. After a while, he found the ground. There was a layer of dirty leaves, some sticks and then nothing but dirt. He cleared an area at the bottom of the snow and set his machine in place.

He had brought along a hose. It was large and solid enough that it could handle some heat. Jerry hooked the hose up to the machine and set it down. Now it was time for phase two of his plan.

He crawled back up to the top of the snow and looked back toward his house. He needed to gauge exactly where his house was from this point.

When he thought he had it all figured out clearly in his mind, he crawled back down, grabbed the hose and started up his heater. It roared to life! He hoped it wasn't too loud for everyone. Jerry could already feel warm air coming out of the end of the hose. Since he had dug all the way down to the ground, he was surrounded on all sides by a wall of snow. Jerry turned the hose toward the wall in the direction of his house and used the heat to melt a hole, creating a snow tunnel.

It was slow progress, but at least he was warm with the heat the machine was creating. In time, he came to a wooden wall, and, sure enough, it was his own house! He had made it through the snow. He looked back and was proud to see a tunnel of ice behind him. Where the snow had melted, it had refrozen as ice. He was happy about this. If he had to make repairs, he could travel back through the tunnel.

Jerry turned his attention back to the house and started to melt more snow. Eventually, he found what he was looking for... a window.

Prying open the shutters and opening the window, he climbed inside and grabbed a small saw. He set to work cutting a small hole in the side of his house, just big enough for the hose to fit in.

Jerry climbed back outside, hooked the hose up to the hole he had just cut and climbed back through the window into the house. He closed up the shutters and stepped back. He could already feel his house warming up. This was going to be a good winter.

The next morning, Jerry woke up feeling warm and cozy. Winter was not going to be so bad if he had his house heated. He was feeling quite happy about this. At least he was happy about the warm and cozy feeling. What he was not happy about was the loud banging sound.

He hopped out of bed, and his feet landed on a warm floor. He smiled at the warm feel of the ground but frowned again as the banging continued. He walked through his warm bedroom and into his warm kitchen. The banging continued. It was coming from outside.

He stared at the door. He could hear someone was out there, banging on the door. Normally, he would just open the door, but he really didn't want to. It was warm in his house, and he thought he would rather not let any cold air in.

"What do you want?" Jerry hollered out to the Squirrel banging on his door.

"We want to know what that noise is! You didn't invent something again, did you? Open the door!"

Jerry was sure that was Mary on the other side of the door. Mary was always a little grumpy in the winter.

"I did invent something. I invented a heater, so I don't have to be so cold," Jerry hollered back.

"What?" Mary called back.

"I invented a house heater," Jerry yelled.

"You sent us a mouse eater?" Mary yelled back. "Why would we need one of those?"

This wasn't working. Jerry had to open the door. Against his better judgment, he grabbed the door handle and turned. He was shocked to see Mary was not alone. About fifteen Squirrels were standing outside his door, and they all quickly poured into his house. He closed the door behind them. He wanted to keep the heat in, but he also wanted to keep more Squirrels from coming in.

"We want to know," Mary began, "what that noise is that we... wait... why is it so warm and cozy in here?"

Everyone looked around, trying to find the source of the heat. They started searching around the house until one of them hollered out, "Found it!"

They huddled around the source of heat, and all tried to soak up as much warmth as possible. Jerry was feeling irritated. He worried that they would like the heat so much, they wouldn't leave. He liked other Squirrels; he just preferred them to be somewhere else.

"Okay, okay, that's enough," Jerry said when he felt they had used enough of his warm air. "I invented a heater for my home for this winter. Maybe next year I can invent one for each of your homes. Soooo... umm... I guess this is good-bye. Thanks for stopping by, everyone."

Jerry hoped they would take the hint. No one moved.

Mary spoke up again. "Jerry. I don't like the cold. Could you hook me up to this heater too?"

Jerry looked at Mary and the other Squirrels. He didn't want to go outside, but he felt bad. No one wanted to be cold all winter. Maybe he could help them out.

"Umm…. I guess I could…" Jerry replied.

Everyone cheered and hugged him. Jerry didn't like the cold. He also didn't like physical contact. He waited until the hugging was done and pushed everyone out of his house, promising them that he would get on heating their houses as soon as possible.

Ten minutes later, he was making his way through the ice tunnel away from his house and toward the heater. He grumbled the whole way. He didn't mind helping everyone out. He actually kind of liked to share his inventions, but he just didn't want to be out in the cold. At least in the tunnel, there was no wind, but he would soon have to go up top.

He arrived at the heater and began his climb. It wasn't hard to climb things, even ice. He was a Squirrel, after all. He climbed out of the hole onto the top of the snow and scampered up a tree. He had brought a little pencil and some paper. He had to map out the town so he could make ice tunnels to everyone's house in the village. Not everyone had asked for the heater, but they would all want it once the small group from earlier told them about their warm houses.

He drew out a map of the homes so he could find the houses under the snow. As he did, he noticed something strange in the distance. It wasn't every day they saw humans up in these woods. Most people avoided Squirrel territory.

He strained to see the three humans walking through the village and realized he recognized each of them. One was Liam. He was the King of Liamville. His friend, Ezra, was walking beside him, and on the other side was a young lady. Her name was DOHNK. They were smiling as they spoke with each other and looked like good friends. He liked it when people smiled. He had felt bad about taking part in the attack on Kings-Home last summer and fighting against those three. He hoped they didn't hold it against him.

He watched them as they walked on, out of sight. They looked like they were pretending not to notice him. That was fine with Jerry.

When Jerry was finished drawing out his map of the village, he scampered back down to the heater and set to work. He attached another hose and started to melt new tunnels in all directions. It seemed to take forever, but he slowly made an ice tunnel network under the snow through to all the houses. He started with Hat Squirrel's house and then moved on to the Squirrels who had visited him that morning. He was right in thinking the others in the village would want the heat. By the time he finished with those who had visited him, all the others had demanded to be hooked up to the central heating.

After he had hooked everyone up, he made his way back home. He was tired, cold and wet from all the melted snow and ice. He wasn't happy. He just wanted to sit in his home and be warm.

He found his house again through the network of ice tunnels and climbed back through the window. He shook off the snow and sat in a chair to warm up. The only problem was, he did not warm up. He went to the heater hose and felt it. There was a little bit of warm air coming through, but not enough to heat a house.

"Of course!" Jerry said, feeling frustrated and disappointed. "The heater wasn't designed for so many houses! I'm going to have to do something to make it produce more heat."

His thoughts were interrupted by a furious banging on the door. He opened it up only to find Mary and the entire village of Erry-Ville pushing their way into his house. He didn't think everyone could fit in, but somehow they managed. Jerry was pinned up against the wall with Mary right next to him. They were eyeball to eyeball. Literally.

Mary was pressed so close to Jerry, the whites of their eyes were actually touching. Jerry did not like this. He found it gross and quite disturbing.

"My house isn't getting warm, Jerry!" Mary said, far too loud considering how close they were to each other. Everyone else chimed in after Mary, telling Jerry they were very upset that the heating they had paid for was not working properly.

Jerry began to explain that they had not, in fact, paid anything for the heating when Hat Squirrel spoke up. "Listen, everyone! Hat Squirrel is speaking which means the rest of you should not be! Jerry! Fix the heat! Do whatever you have to in order to make our houses warm! Make them warm by midnight tonight, or I'm going to banish you from Erry-Ville, forever!"

The door opened, and all the Squirrels filed out of his house. Jerry's shoulder's sunk, and he lowered his head. He had to figure this one out. He returned to his desk and began to think. It didn't take long before he came up with a design for a turbocharger.

He set to work immediately, and within an hour, he had it figured out. It took another half-hour to build it, and in no time he was out at the heater hooking it up. It was only about nine o'clock at night, so he had plenty of time before he would be banished. He didn't like the sound of being banished.

It only took a few minutes to get it all set up. He had built the turbocharger in such a way that it would only kick in if it were needed. It would wait until more heat was needed, then it would kick in and send more heat to the houses. He wasn't sure how much heat it would produce, but he thought it couldn't be too much heat.

He rushed back to his house, anxious to start feeling warm again. It was pretty dark outside and the night was much colder than the day had been. He climbed inside and wandered over to the hose.

Not much heat was coming out. That was okay. The turbocharger would kick in shortly. He waited another moment and began to worry that his turbo-charger wouldn't work, but then he heard it. It kicked in with a roar. Any moment now, the heat would come pouring in, and his house would be cozy again.

He was right. It didn't take long for heat to come. Unfortunately, the heat that came was in the form of fire.

He didn't realize his turbo-charger was that powerful. Flames shot out of the hose in the wall, and he yelled out!

Jerry sprang into action and dove out the window. He rolled on the icy ground once or twice and then got to his feet, racing to the heater. He arrived in no time and hit the off switch. He was pretty sure he had gotten it turned off fast enough that none of the houses would have caught on fire.

He was cold again. Very cold. He was very cold and very unhappy. He looked down, wondering why he was so cold and realized he had a big problem. The fire had burnt every bit of hair off his body. He squeaked in embarrassment and ran as fast as he could back to his house. He climbed back in the window and looked around for something to cover himself with. The only thing that came to mind was to use the leaves he had in his walls for insulation.

He pulled them out in handfuls and grabbed a needle and thread. Sewing them together, he made himself a quick pair of pants. He finished just in time, as there was a loud, angry banging sound on the door.

He opened the door, a little worried about what he might see. His worst fears had come true. Every Squirrel in the village stood before him. Each one wearing an outfit sewed out of insulation leaves. Not one of them looked happy with Jerry.

Jerry knew this was going to be a long, cold winter.

Rental Part I

Jerry was a Squirrel. Jerry was also an inventor... quite a good one, as a matter of fact. He could design and build just about anything. The problem was, Jerry's inventions rarely worked the way he wanted them to work.

Jerry was hungry. He didn't normally feel hungry, but he hadn't been eating much lately.

It was getting close to nut harvest time and he, unfortunately, had not saved up enough nuts to carry him through until the new nuts were ready. This often happened to Squirrels, but never before to Jerry. He had always been careful and planned so well, but this year he had just not been careful enough.

He had realized he didn't have enough nuts about two weeks earlier and had started to eat less in the hopes of making his supply last. It would be another month before the fresh nuts would be ready. This had left him very hungry, and he started to realize that even if he ate less, he would still run out before it was harvest time.

At first, he tried to get himself invited over to the houses of other Squirrels so they would feed him. He did this with Terry, but then Terry asked if he could come over to Jerry's house the next night. He didn't want to be rude, so he invited Terry and his family over. Terry ate a lot. His family ate more. Now Jerry didn't have many nuts left at all.

He looked down into his bin where he kept his food, and he realized he only had enough for two more days. Terry and his family sure did eat a lot.

He had to come up with a new idea. He didn't feel that he wanted to starve, so he figured he should find some way to get some food. He thought about selling some inventions, but few Squirrels ever really trusted his inventions enough to pay for them. He thought about doing some work for some other Squirrels. He thought maybe he could do some of Mary's gardening, but when he asked her, she chased him off her property. She didn't like Squirrels near her garden.

As he stared down into the bin of food and wondered how he could get some more food, he thought of something. He had a way to get some food! He could rent out his apartment upstairs!

He ran outside and to the stairs on the side of his house. They led up to the apartment, and he ran up the steps, opened the apartment door and ran inside. He hadn't been in the apartment for many weeks, and he took a good look around. It was in great shape. It looked really nice, and as he looked out the windows, he could see a wonderful view of Erry-Ville!

He thought it through and realized that he could rent out the apartment for enough nuts to feed him right through until harvest! This was his answer!

He ran back downstairs and grabbed a piece of paper. He quickly drew up a little poster to advertise his apartment and ran out with the poster, a hammer and a nail into the center of town. There was a small tree growing right in the middle of all the houses, and he used his hammer to nail up his poster.

Jerry walked back to his apartment with a big smile on his face. He thought to himself about all the nuts he would have as soon as someone came and rented his apartment! This was going to be tasty!

He ran back to his house and sat down at his desk. He knew he just needed to wait a little bit and someone would knock on his door.

He waited. He waited some more. He waited and waited and waited. Soon, the sun began to set, and he realized no one was coming that night.

Jerry wandered over to his bed and settled in for the night. He was hungry... so hungry... and hoped tomorrow would bring a renter to him.

The next morning Jerry rose out of bed and wandered into the kitchen. He drank a lot of water and ate some nuts. He wondered if maybe his poster had fallen off the tree and was about to head out to check on it when there was a knock on his door.

Jerry opened up the door to see not just one Squirrel standing outside, but a line-up of Squirrels! He was so excited, he could almost taste the nuts he was about to get!

The first one in line was Mary. He thought that was odd as Mary had a house—quite a nice one as a matter of fact—and he couldn't see why she would want to rent his apartment. They sat down at the table in his kitchen.

"Hi, Mary." Jerry thought this was a great way to start a conversation.

"Let's skip the pleasantries, Jerry!" Mary replied. "I want to rent your upstairs apartment."

"Okay. That sounds good, Mary," Jerry said. He didn't mind skipping the pleasantries with Mary. She was always a hard one to talk to.

"I want to rent your apartment for my plants," Mary explained. "I will give you one nut a month, so I can store all my plants up in your apartment for the winter. They will require lots of dirt so we will have to fill your apartment with soil and I'll want to water it every day."

"Won't that ruin my apartment?" Jerry asked. "And to ruin my apartment for only one nut a month seems like a bad idea to me." Jerry didn't like where this was all going.

"It sounds like a great idea to me!" Mary said as she stood up and put her hands on her hips. She looked crossly at Jerry and said, "I don't think you're being very considerate. Think about how much this will help me and how much I want this."

"I can see that, but if you're watering it every day, where is the water going to go?" Jerry asked. He knew the plants would take some of it, but what if the extra water poured down on him in his house below?

"I would think that it would pour down on you in your house below!" she said. "That might be a bit of a sacrifice for you, but I think that's something you should be willing to do for me." Jerry wasn't sure how, but Mary managed to look even more crossly at him.

"Why don't you do this in your house?" Jerry asked.

"What?" Mary shouted. "That could ruin my house! Besides, it would make my house all musty, and there could be mold! I'm not doing that in my house! That's why I want to do it in yours. Since I'm offering a full nut a month, you'd think you would be grateful!" Once again, she managed to look even more crossly at Jerry. Mary's face was so scrunched up, Jerry began to wonder if her face was going to cave in on itself.

"I think I'm going to talk to the rest of the Squirrels outside before I make my decision," Jerry explained as he stood up and led her to the door.

The next Squirrel to come in was Larry. Jerry wondered why he would want to rent the upstairs apartment. Larry also didn't need a place to stay. He had quite a nice house, not too far from Mary's house.

They walked into Jerry's kitchen and sat down at the table. Jerry was just about to say, "Hi Larry," when Larry cut him off.

"Okay, now that the pleasantries are out of the way, here's the deal," Larry began. He looked really excited. "I'm offering you an opportunity of a lifetime. I will give you as many nuts as you want a month if I can rent your upstairs apartment for me and my friends."

Jerry wasn't sure what Larry was talking about. "What do you mean? Who are your friends? What are you thinking of using the apartment for?"

"Jerry," Larry began, "this is really exciting. You can't wait to hear what I have to tell you. Are you sitting down?"

"Yes, I would think you could see that. I'm sitting right in front of you," Jerry replied.

"Never mind that. This is important. You may not know this about me, but I'm the president of the local civil war re-enactment guild." Larry had a big smile on his face. "I don't tell Squirrels about it because I know they would all want my autograph, but I have to tell you if I'm to give you such a great opportunity."

"I can see how the fame would be a big worry of yours," Jerry replied, still a little unsure where this was going.

Larry leaned in close. "I'm about to blow your socks off!" He looked down at Jerry's feet. "Okay, I would, if you were wearing socks. Here's what I want to do for you. I'm going to rent your apartment so that my friends and I can hold our weekly meetings in your upstairs apartment. Not only that, we will actually be able to hold our re-enactments upstairs! This means you would be hosting re-enactments of the civil war every single week in your upstairs apartment! How awesome is that???"

"Did we even have a civil war?" Jerry asked.

"I know! That's exactly what I asked when I first heard about it, but then I decided not to ask too many questions, and I just went with it." Larry had a big grin on his face and looked so proud of himself.

"So, this civil war re-enactment that you want to do... tell me about it." Jerry was a little worried about what this would do to his apartment.

"Well, we have about eighty Squirrels that get together. We run around with some old guns and a few old canons and battle it out like they did back in the day!" Larry explained.

"I see," Jerry said, although he wasn't sure he actually did. "You know that my apartment's really small, right? And what's this about firing off canons in my apartment? Won't that blow a hole in the side of my house?"

"Oh, I expect that'll blow many holes in the side of your house, Jerry. They're pretty amazing canons!" Larry said.

"I think this might not be the best fit, Larry. I have some other Squirrels to talk to." With that, he led Larry to the front door and called in the next person.

Most of the Squirrels who followed didn't seem to be any better. Many wanted to do things with his apartment that would destroy it and his entire house. They all had houses of their own; they just preferred to do the damage to his house rather than their own. One guy wanted to use the house as storage for his collection of decomposing leaves. One lady wanted to use his apartment for aerobics classes every morning, afternoon and three times throughout the night. Hat Squirrel even wanted to use his apartment for his gymnastics club to use. At first, Jerry thought this was the best option of all, until he found out they only practiced their gymnastics at nighttime from midnight to seven.

Finally, there was only one last Squirrel.

She was old. She was very old. She walked with a little cane and wore spectacles on her face. She was a little hunched over and wore a shawl draped over her shoulders. As she came in, she looked up at Jerry with a sweet smile on her face.

She spoke to him in a gentle, kind, grandmotherly voice. "Hello, dear, my name is Sherry. It is good to meet you. You have a lovely home, here. Would you like some cookies?"

She handed a plate of freshly baked nut cookies to Jerry. They smelled delicious, and they were still warm! He raced back to the table and took a bite of one of them. He was so hungry, and they tasted so very good.

He looked up at the lady and smiled back at her as she sat down. "Hello, Sherry, my name is Jerry."

"Yes, dear, I saw that on the poster. It is so very good to finally meet you. You are such a nice, polite, young Squirrel." She smiled again. She looked just about as sweet as the cookies she had baked.

Jerry looked down at the empty plate. He still felt hungry, but it was so good to have his belly partly full.

"I can't pay you very much, I'm just a poor old Squirrel, but I think I can pay enough. I would like to rent your upstairs apartment. Would that be okay, dear?"

After eating the warm, freshly baked cookies, he almost yelled out, "Yes!" but knew that he needed to be careful. He had just met so many Squirrels who had so many weird things they wanted to do with his house! "Um, do you do gymnastics?"

"Dear, I haven't done gymnastics in a long, long time." She smiled sweetly again.

"Are you planning on doing civil war re-enactments in my house? Shooting canons? Storing plants and filling the apartment with dirt and pouring water on them?" Jerry asked.

"No, dear. I think maybe you hit your head or something, dear," she said sweetly. "Are you listening to yourself? Did we even have a civil war?" She smiled again. "I just want to rent the apartment to live there."

Jerry chuckled. "I guess those must seem like odd questions. Yes, you can rent the apartment."

The woman smiled again and took his hand. "You seem stressed, dear. Can I sing you a lullaby?"

"Um, sure," Jerry said. He had had a rough day, and this lady was the sweetest Squirrel he had ever met.

She pulled out some knitting needles and began to knit while she sang. He felt himself relax. Every muscle in his body seemed to turn to jelly. He felt so happy and at such peace.

When she finished, he looked at her and handed her a piece of paper. It was the rental agreement to say she could rent it for a year. He was so happy to have found someone as sweet as Sherry.

Once they had signed the agreement, the old lady Squirrel stood up to leave. She smiled again at him and said she would be back the next day.

Jerry walked her to the door, and as she was leaving, he thanked her again for the cookies. "They were very good," he said. A thought struck him. "Hey, if you were waiting out here all day to see me, how did you bring me freshly baked cookies?"

"Oh, dear, I just bought them down at the corner store and brought them up to you. They weren't freshly baked," she said.

"But they were still warm! How were they still warm?" Jerry asked, feeling quite confused.

"Oh, I was sitting on them, dear," she said as she turned and made her way down the path.

Jerry thought that was odd, but hoped that was the oddest thing that he had to face with her. He hoped she would still bring him cookies, although he found it gross that she was sitting on them. He thought maybe he could ask her not to do that.

The next day, she arrived with a small bag. Jerry took her upstairs and gave her a key to the apartment. She climbed the stairs slowly, using her cane for support. She didn't have much with her but told him the rest of her things would arrive soon.

After she had settled in, Jerry walked out the door, down the stairs and slammed into a wall of fur. Jerry fell backward onto the ground and looked up at the creature before him. It was a mountain of a Squirrel. The Squirrel standing before him was huge! He looked mean and cruel and like he could pick up Jerry's entire house with one hand. He also smelled. Not just a little bit, but like he had never had a single bath in his entire life. Ever. Jerry wasn't sure he had ever smelled anything quite like it in his life.

The mountain of a Squirrel leaned down until his face was only a short distance from Jerry's face. He opened his mouth and said in a deep, powerful and airy voice, "Hiiiiiiiii! I'm Gary."

Jerry now realized Gary's breath was far worse than the rest of his smell. He started to see spots and was afraid he would pass out, but managed to scoot back a little bit on his butt and get some fresh air.

"Hi, Gary, I'm Jerry," he said through coughs and gags. "Is there anything I can help you with?"

"Hi, Jerry. I don't think you can help me with anything. I live here," Gary said, smiling a huge smile.

"Um, no, I don't think you do. I live here. This is my house," Jerry said.

"No, Jerry. I mean I live with my mom. Her name is Sherry. She lives upstairs."

With that, he stepped around Jerry and started up the stairs. Jerry looked around at the stairs in fear. He listened to them creak and moan under the weight of the giant Squirrel and wondered if the stairs could hold him.

Jerry got to his feet and began to worry. He didn't know that Sherry had a son and that he would be living with her. Gary was huge. Jerry thought he would be able to hear every step that Squirrel took above his head.

He ran into his house to listen. He was right. He could hear every step. He could also hear Sherry's cane every time she used it on the floor. It was like a hammer hitting the floor each time.

After about fifteen minutes of hearing every step from Gary sounding like the beat of a drum and the sound of the cane beating on the floor as Sherry walked, he heard Sherry holler out loudly, "Gary! When I was talking to Jerry yesterday, he gave me an idea! I haven't done gymnastics in a long time! Let's practice!"

Jerry wasn't sure the ceiling would hold. He quickly ran around the house and braced the ceiling with boards and beams and anything he could find on short notice. He envisioned the entire house coming down.

He finished just in time to hear the crashes and bangs of Sherry and Gary's gymnastics.

To be continued…

Rental Part II

Sherry and Gary continued with their gymnastics all through the day and late into the evening. Jerry wasn't sure how Sherry could manage to jump and roll and bounce around the apartment at her age. Jerry wondered how someone who used a cane could move like that!

But Sherry wasn't the biggest worry. Gary jumped and rolled and bounced just like Jerry would have expected someone of his size to jump and roll and bounce. He did it loudly.

By the time they finished, it was late in the day. Jerry was quite tired and quite ready for bed. He crawled under his sheets and closed his eyes. Everything was quiet, and he was sure he would be sound asleep in no time.

That's when it started.

A roar sounded and echoed across Erry-ville. Jerry ran out of his house and stood on the road, looking all around. He feared they were under attack.

He wondered if Kenny the Dragon had arrived. Kenny was usually such a nice guy, but he could get grumpy if he had a head cold. Maybe Hat Squirrel had upset him again, and Kenny was here for revenge.

The roar sounded again, and the very trees around Jerry's home shook.

Again and again, the roar echoed through the trees. Jerry turned this way and that and ran every which way he could. He ran up and down the streets looking for the source of the sound. He didn't really want to face Kenny or any creature that could make that noise, but he knew if they were under attack, he had to do something.

Finally, he stopped and decided to use his brain a little bit. He listened to the roar as it continued, over and over again. He turned in the direction of the roar and slowly started to make his way toward it. He moved slowly so he wouldn't lose his direction and walk away from the sound again.

As he walked, the sound grew louder, and he was surprised to find the sound was loudest near his house. He realized the sound must be coming from behind his house, so he ran around back. When he arrived at the back of the house, there was nothing there to cause such a roar.

He stopped again and turned around with fear in his heart. He finally knew what was going on, and it was far worse than he could have imagined. He would almost prefer an attack by Kenny. He would prefer to be under attack by the frog creatures of the Aron Mountains. He would prefer to be in a one on one battle with a full-sized Bodal warrior. He would prefer just about anything to the truth of what was going on.

It was Gary. He knew it must be Gary. Gary was a snorer. Not just any snorer, but Gary was a powerful snorer. He sounded as if Kenny the Dragon was actually stuck up his nose and desperately trying to get out.

Jerry walked back into his house feeling very sorry for himself. He feared he would never sleep again.

The next morning, Jerry woke up. That in itself was a good sign. It meant he had in fact fallen asleep at some point.

The upsetting part of waking up, however, was how he woke up. It wasn't the sun shining through his window or the sound of birds chirping. It wasn't the smell of pancakes or coffee brewing in the kitchen. It wasn't anything which might cause him to gently wake up.

It was, sadly, Gary. It turned out Gary played the trumpet.

When Gary started playing the trumpet, it scared Jerry so much he leapt out of his bed and found himself clinging with all his strength to one of the beams on the ceiling. He looked around again like he was under attack, but as he looked over at the window, he could see the belly of a very large Squirrel.

Jerry let himself down and walked to the window. He opened it up and leaned out.

"Hi, Jerry! I'm Gary. I live here in your upstairs apartment," Gary said with a big smile. He then reached out and pulled Jerry right through the window and gave him a big hug. "Thanks for being such a good friend."

"Um, you're welcome, Gary. Why are you playing the trumpet so early in the morning?"

"Oh, I'm glad you asked! I play it in the morning because it would be rude to play it at nighttime while everyone is trying to sleep. That's a time when you should be quiet," Gary explained.

"Yes, I believe you're right about that," Jerry said.

Jerry hung there in the air. Gary seemed to have forgotten that he was still hugging Jerry and showed no sign of ending the hug anytime soon.

"Do you think maybe the afternoon might be a better time to play the trumpet? It doesn't have to be very early in the morning," Jerry asked.

"Oh, I don't mind playing in the morning, but thanks for asking," Gary replied before dropping Jerry and going back to his playing.

By this time, Sherry had managed to come down the stairs. She was holding a bag full of nuts out to Jerry. "This isn't quite the full month's rent, but I wanted to give you a little bit now. I'll be getting the rest to you tomorrow, dear," she said sweetly. "Thank you again for such a wonderful apartment. We love it so much. I think, though, you should get those floors looked at. I don't think they are as strong as you thought. You probably shouldn't have recommended we practice gymnastics."

"I didn't," Jerry explained. "Where did you learn gymnastics anyway?"

"Oh, sweetie, I learned gymnastics as part of my training for being a gladiator when I was a little younger."

Jerry didn't think that was a thing. Squirrels didn't train to be gladiators, did they? He looked to see if she was joking, but she just continued to smile sweetly back at him.

Jerry noticed she was also carrying a plate of cookies which she then handed to him. "Here you go, dear. These are for you."

Jerry felt them, and they were warm. He looked at her with suspicion. "Did you sit on these to make them warm?"

"What? Oh no, dear, of course not. I don't sit on cookies unless I have to. Go ahead and eat them."

Jerry did, and they were fantastic. He was really having a hard time knowing how to respond to these two. They were so loud, but they were both so nice. Not only that, but he loved the cookies she kept giving him.

When he had finished, he handed the empty plate back to her. "Thanks, Sherry, they were really tasty."

"You're welcome, dear. Gary was so pleased to be able to warm them up for you this morning. He sat on them for an hour before coming down to wake you up with his beautiful song." Sherry smiled again at Jerry.

Jerry's stomach began to turn and then his ears began to hurt as Gary started to play his trumpet again. The new song he was playing was a rendition of a single note being played over and over again.

Jerry had an idea. Jerry had a great idea. Jerry smiled as he realized he was about to invent something.

He ran into his house and got right to work. He sat at his desk and grabbed a piece of paper. He usually started by drawing out his plan. He found that was the best way to go. Inventing with a plan drawn out ahead of time allowed him to keep in mind where he was going with his invention. It also helped to remind him what he was inventing if he ever started to daydream.

He finished his drawing and held it up so he could see it. The invention looked good. He had all the supplies sitting out before him, and he was sure he could finish it in no time.

He set himself to work at assembling his invention. Every now and then he had to check to make sure it was the right size or the right weight. He had to experiment with it to make sure it worked just as he wanted it to.

In the end, it only took him a few hours to put it all together, but he was done. Jerry had invented a set of earplugs which would keep all the annoying sounds such as trumpets, snoring and gymnastics out of his head, but would allow all the good sounds such as birds chirping or the sound of gentle winds blowing through the trees to come through. He named his invention, "Peace."

As he stood up from his desk, he looked out the window and was surprised to see that it was dark outside. He had been working all day, and it was time for bed.

The roar began. Gary had obviously fallen asleep.

Jerry smiled to himself and wandered over to his bed. He laid down with his head back against the pillow and listened to Gary's snore for a moment before he raised the earplugs up to his head and put them in.

Instantly the snore was gone. Jerry was so surprised with how well they worked that he thought maybe Gary had actually stopped snoring. He pulled the earplugs from his ears and sure enough, Gary was still snoring.

Jerry put the plugs back in, and the horrible sound disappeared. All he could hear was the sound of a gentle breeze outside, rustling the leaves and the occasional cricket chirp, sounding out through the nighttime air. The earplugs worked. He could hear only peace.

The next morning he opened his eyes, feeling well rested and happy. The only sounds he could hear were, again, the normal sounds. Birds were chirping, the wind was blowing gently through the trees, and the gentle sound of raindrops falling through the leaves and on the roof of his house could be heard.

It was a great morning and a great way to wake up. Jerry sat up and pulled the earplugs out of his ears. He didn't realize until that moment that Gary was playing his trumpet right outside his bedroom window! The sound hit Jerry so hard he rolled off the side of his bed and crawled under the bed to hide before he realized he was in no danger.

Gary's song this morning consisted of two notes: a very high note and a very low note. He would play one, then the other. He would then start back at the beginning and play the one note, then the other. Jerry quickly put his earplugs back in and went about his business.

He grabbed some breakfast and stepped outside. It was raining, but Arestanian Squirrels do not mind the rain. Rain kept the Squirrels clean, and they enjoyed playing in the mud.

As Jerry walked down the road, he continued to enjoy the peaceful sounds of the rain slowly coming down as well as the wind gently blowing through the trees. This was a good day.

He noticed as well that the plugs seemed to be filtering out some of what the other Squirrels were saying. Larry walked by and said, "Good morning, Jerry." Jerry heard him loud and clear. As he walked by Mary's house, he noticed she had her hands on her hips, and her mouth was moving very fast. She looked like she was scolding someone, and she was looking at Jerry. Jerry figured he was probably the one she was scolding, but he couldn't hear a word she said. The earplugs worked perfectly! He smiled at her, nodded and walked on.

As he walked along with the rain pouring down on his head, he suddenly had a sharp pain in both ears. It was as if the earplugs had short-circuited and shocked him. He reached up, rubbed around his ears and adjusted the plugs a little bit. His ears felt fine, and he could still hear the pleasant sound of the gentle rain and the breeze slowly blowing through the trees. Now and then a bird would chirp. He felt so relaxed.

Jerry continued his walk around the town but noticed Squirrels around him were not acting the way they normally acted. He found he couldn't hear any of them. He was fine with this as he felt they would only say something irritating, but thought he should be careful as they appeared to be running around in a panic.

Something deep inside him told him that he should take out the earplugs to see what was going on. He wondered if perhaps they needed help, and he could solve their problem. He wondered if maybe Erry-Ville was in danger, or if there was a catastrophe happening at that very moment.

He then began to notice that some of the Squirrels were running around with their hands covering their ears and had a look of pain on their faces. He realized immediately what the problem must be. Gary must be taking a nap, and everyone was suffering from the sound of his snoring. It was pretty loud.

He noticed Harry and Kerri run by. They looked like they were in agony. He noticed Larry and Barrie run by. They looked like they were looking for a place to hide. He saw Hat Squirrel off in the distance. He appeared to be wrapping leaves around his ears and trying to pull the hat down, so it covered his whole head.

He was thinking Gary's snoring must be especially bad today when he noticed Sherry standing at the end of the road. She was in tears and in her arms was a giant

Squirrel. It was Gary. He was weeping, and Sherry was holding him, cradling him like he was a baby.

It was an odd sight. Sherry was such a tiny Squirrel and quite elderly. Gary, her son, was a massive Squirrel. The fact that she could lift him at all and cradle him in her arms at all was impressive! It was also a little disturbing to see such a huge Squirrel crying like a baby.

As odd as this was, it did tell Jerry one thing. Gary was not the reason everyone was running in fear.

It was time to find out what was going on. Jerry pulled out his earplugs and immediately put them back in. The noise was terrible. In that short second, while his earplugs were out of his ears, he thought he heard every sound ever made in Erry-Ville ever since the beginning of time, all at once and all very loud.

He slowly pulled them out again. He had to figure out what was going on.

The sound was loud, but through the noise, he could start to make out what kinds of sounds he was hearing. He was, in fact, hearing loud snoring. This was strange as it sounded like Gary, but Gary was crying in his mother's arms.

He could also hear Gary playing the trumpet. Again, this didn't make sense. He could also hear Mary screaming something about her garden and how Jerry was getting too close to her poison ivy or some such plant. Jerry had never paid too much attention to plant life. What was really strange about that was Mary was standing on her front lawn, just a short distance away. She had her hands over her ears, and her lips were pressed tightly together. She was not screaming at anyone.

Jerry could also hear Hat Squirrel yelling orders to everyone to stop making so much noise. He kept saying, "I'm Hat Squirrel! I'm in charge here! This noise must stop!" Hat Squirrel, however, by this point, had curled himself up in a little ball on the ground. He wasn't speaking or moving or doing anything for that matter. He was just lying there.

The sound was hurting Jerry's ears, and he knew he had to put a stop to it really soon. He wanted to put the earplugs back in, but then he knew he would not be able to find the source of the sound.

He started to run. He figured he would run until the sound grew louder and then he would know he was getting close to it. If it grew quieter, he would know he was getting farther away.

He ran and ran and ran. He ran up one street and down another. He ran into his house and out again. He even ran across Mary's lawn. He didn't think he needed to do that, but she didn't seem to be paying attention, and he wanted to see what it was like. It turned out it was no different than anyone else's lawn.

He decided to stop and think, so he came to a halt. He put the earplugs back in, and the sound died out immediately. He concentrated.

He realized the sounds he had been hearing were all the sounds the Squirrels had been making in the last number of hours. It obviously included the nighttime because one of the sounds was Gary and his snoring. It also included the sound of Mary scolding him and many Squirrels talking. It included all those sounds, but just very loud.

He also started to think that the sound was the same volume everywhere he went. That was strange. He knew there must be a reason for that because sound didn't normally act that way. It would normally be loud at the source and quieter the farther away you ran from it.

That's when he started to realize the problem. The source of the sound was following him.

He looked down at his body. He was just wearing his normal fur that he wore every day. His glasses couldn't make that kind of sound. Nothing was different about him today except for one thing—his earplugs.

He pulled them off and cringed at the sound. It was just as loud and just as annoying as it had been the last time he took them off.

As he looked closely at them, he could see they were sparking a little bit. The rain was causing the earplugs to short circuit! Somehow, it was taking all the sounds it was filtering out for Jerry and loudly broadcasting them out across the entire village of Erry-Ville!

He didn't know what to do about it. He couldn't keep them, but then he didn't want to have to listen to Gary snoring every night and playing the trumpet every morning! He had to figure out what to do!

A shadow passed over him, and he looked up to see Gary standing there. He had tears in his eyes. "Jerry?

What's making that loud noise? It's hurting my ears? Can you fix it?"

With that, Gary burped. Not just any burp, but a loud one. Not just any loud burp, but a burp so loud it was a burp to end all burps.

The burp continued, and Jerry could feel the wind from it pass over him and blow his fur back. He felt himself slip a little bit in the mud and tried to dig his claws into the ground to keep himself in one place. The burp continued to blast in his direction, and Jerry realized the volume was louder than Gary's snoring and trumpet playing combined. The smell, too, was horrible. Jerry thought he could smell just about every meal Gary had ever eaten... all at once. The burp didn't seem to be capable of coming to an end. It was as if it had a life of its own, or it had simply forgotten how to stop.

When the burp finally ended, Jerry wondered to himself how much time had passed. He briefly considered looking down at his fur to see if he had gone gray during that time, but realized that much time couldn't have passed. At most, it could have been a day.

"I'm sorry, Jerry. Sometimes I burp when I'm upset," Gary explained, looking a little embarrassed. "Hey, it's quiet again!"

Jerry realized it was. The earplugs were silent. They were no longer broadcasting every sound at high volume. Maybe Gary's burp had fixed them.

Jerry looked down at the earplugs. The earplugs were sparking and shaking. At first, Jerry wasn't sure what to make of it, but then his heart went cold. The earplugs were still broadcasting all the sounds, they just weren't prepared for Gary's burp. They were processing the volume and the pitch and preparing to let loose!

When it started, the ground itself shook. The ground was wet and muddy, and Jerry feared a mudslide would begin due to the volume of the belch. Both Jerry and Gary were knocked over by the sheer force of the sound from the earplugs. It was Gary's burp, just a hundred times louder.

Jerry knew what he had to do. He had to destroy the earplugs. If he didn't, he wasn't sure any of them would survive. In the blast of sound, Jerry had dropped the earplugs. He could see them in the mud where he had been standing before the mega-belch had begun to broadcast.

He grabbed hold of a root sticking up out of the ground to keep himself in place. He looked around and saw that in the massive sound being produced by his earplugs, Squirrels had begun to fly through the air. The sound was blowing Squirrels off into the distance. Even Gary was rolling away.

Jerry was their last hope. He had to make it to the earplugs if they were ever to live in Erry-Ville again.

He pulled himself forward, forcing himself to move against the rush of sound and wind flowing from the Mega-Belch. He was almost there. Only a few more inches and he would be near the earplugs. With one last pull on the root, he was there. He grabbed hold of the earplugs. They were shaking, and somehow they continued to broadcast such a terrible sound.

Jerry looked around for a rock or something to use to smash the earplugs in the hopes of putting an end to their reign of terror. There was nothing. Because of the rain, the ground was all soft and muddy.

There had to be some way to stop the sound. He looked down at them in the hopes of finding a way to destroy them with his bare hands. He squeezed and pulled and twisted as the Mega-Belch continued, but he could not break them.

He was about to give up and run for cover when he noticed something on the side of one of the earplugs. There was a tiny switch. He remembered something about installing a switch, but he could not remember what it was for.

He looked at the tiny words by the tiny switch. One side read, "Filter Normal." That made sense. The other side read, "Filter and Broadcast." That didn't make sense. The switch was currently set to "Filter and Broadcast." Jerry couldn't remember installing that feature but thought he would try it out. He switched the earplugs from "Filter and Broadcast" to "Filter Normal."

The Mega-Belch stopped. It all stopped. All the sound. All except the normal, peaceful sounds of the gentle rain and the wind blowing through the trees. He realized that he must have accidentally switched it from one setting to another without noticing while he was out for his walk in the rain.

He looked around and saw no one else. The blast from the Mega-Belch must have blown them far away.

Hat Squirrel was going to be mad. Hat Squirrel was going to be very mad. Jerry realized everyone would be very mad. He really didn't want to face them after this.

At first, he wasn't sure what to do, but then he had an idea. He realized they probably didn't know the earplugs were the source of the sound. They probably didn't even know there were earplugs.

Jerry quickly ran back to his house and dropped the earplugs on the desk, making sure the setting was still where it should be. He then ran out into the streets and off into the woods. When he noticed a group of Squirrels wandering back toward the village, he ran quietly around a tree and joined up with them.

Larry was up front, talking as he made his way back to the village. "That was quite the burp! I'm sure whoever burped like that must have a sore throat now. I hope everyone's okay."

He noticed Jerry. "Hey Jerry," Larry said. "I see you survived the burp too."

Jerry looked at Larry for a moment before replying. "Yup. Terrible thing, that burp. Noisy day, for sure."

Gary Smell

Jerry was a Squirrel. Jerry was also an inventor... quite a good one, as a matter of fact. He could design and build just about anything. The problem was, Jerry's inventions rarely worked the way he wanted them to work.

Jerry jumped out of bed in terror. He didn't know what was going on. All he knew was there was a horrible sound echoing throughout his house.

He covered his ears and ran out of the bedroom and into the kitchen. He looked around for what could be making the noise and found there was nothing out of the ordinary.

He ran outside, and the sound was just as loud in front of his house, but still no sign of what was causing the noise. He looked right and left and up and down and still he had no idea where the noise could possibly be coming from.

Jerry stopped himself and decided he'd better think this one through. He closed his eyes and asked himself if he had ever heard the sound before. He realized he had. He could remember hearing this noise every morning for the last couple of months, and each morning it shocked him.

He continued to cover his ears as he walked around the side of the house to see Gary from the upstairs apartment, standing just outside Jerry's bedroom window. He was playing his trumpet. It was loud.

Gary had two songs. The first one was a song that was just one note. Gary would play that note over and over and over and over again. The second song was much better. There were two notes. Gary would play the one, then the other. Then he would play the first note again, then the other.

Gary also had a strong odor to himself that was not very nice. He had breath that kind of smelled like rotting leaves and fur that smelled like he had been rolling around in those leaves.

"Good morning, Jerry. It's good to see you. I wanted to wake you up with a new song I've been working on. It has a note that I play really loudly, over and over and over again," Gary said with a big smile on his face.

"How is this song any different than your other one-note song?" Jerry asked.

"Well," Gary explained, "this song is played louder than my old song with just one note. I still play the same note, but when I play it, I have to blow as hard as I can. Sometimes I blow so hard, spit comes out the end of the trumpet."

As if to show Jerry what he meant, Gary blew the trumpet as hard and as loud as he could in Jerry's face. Gary was right; spit did come out the end of the trumpet.

"Thanks, Gary," Jerry said as he wiped the spittle from his face. "I think you're right. You do blow very hard through that trumpet. Do you think maybe you could not do that first thing in the morning? It's really loud."

"What's wrong with first thing in the morning?" Gary asked, looking very confused.

"It wakes me up and scares me. Each morning I come running out of the house in fear as if something is going to attack me. I prefer to wake up to something more gentle," Jerry answered.

"Ahh, I see what you mean," Gary replied. "I have the perfect solution. No worries. Tomorrow will be better." With that, he turned and walked away, playing his new song as loud as he could.

Jerry went back into his house and had some breakfast. Today he had some work to do on a new invention he was working on.

He had been awakened every morning for the last long while to the sound of Gary and his trumpet playing. Jerry needed a break from the noise, so he had been working on a way to soundproof his house. He had most of the walls done, but there was a little bit more to do. He also had to install the window and door coverings. They were large, thick, wooden boards, covered in leaves and moss to keep out the sound.

He had designed it so that when the noise would start up, he could just press a button right next to his bed, and large coverings would slam down over his windows and door and prevent all sound from coming in. He didn't like the idea of turning his house into a fortress to keep out all sound, but he couldn't keep being awakened by the sound of horribleness every morning.

Jerry worked all day and into the evening, and by the time he was done, he was ready for bed. He couldn't wait to try out his plan for the next morning.

Jerry had told Gary the Squirrel that he didn't like the trumpet playing in the morning and Gary said he had a solution, but Jerry didn't want to learn what it was. He just wanted quiet.

He walked over to his bed and looked at the button on the wall. It was perfect. When Jerry would lie on the bed, it would be just in the right spot so he could reach over, press the button and the window coverings would slam down.

He was proud of the button. He didn't want an ugly button right next to his bed. He thought that would not look nice, but he didn't know what to do at first. Then he had an idea. He decided to make the button into the shape of a nut. Then it would look like it fit perfectly in a Squirrel home! He was pleased with it.

He decided he should probably test it out before the morning came. He lay down on his bed and reached over to press the button. He was excited. Maybe this would solve the noise problem once and for all!

He listened for a moment to all the sounds he could hear. They were nice sounds—the sounds of nighttime. Birds were singing night songs. Crickets were chirping. There was the sound of some Squirrels scurrying along outside his house on one of the paths. It felt good to hear such nice, peaceful sounds.

It was time to test out the soundproofing he had installed. Jerry pressed the button and watched as the coverings slammed down over the window. He looked at the window by his bed and the one by his desk. Both were covered. He ran out into the kitchen and, sure enough, the window and door were both sealed tight.

He ran back to his bed, jumped in and listened. There was no sound of birds. There was no sound of crickets. There was no sound of Squirrels scurrying by.

He liked those sounds, but since he couldn't hear them it told him that his soundproofing had worked! He cheered really loudly. Normally he would be quiet at nighttime, so he didn't wake the neighbors, but there was no need when the soundproofing was working. He could be as loud as he wanted.

He pressed the button again, and the coverings pulled back and uncovered the door and windows. He could hear the pleasant night sounds again.

Jerry tested the button out a few more times, just to make sure it worked perfectly. Each time he pressed it, the coverings would quickly slam down and then when he pressed it again, they would return to their spot up on the ceiling of his house.

It worked. He would not have to suffer from Gary's trumpet playing anymore.

He made sure the windows and door were uncovered so he could fall asleep with the sound of the birds singing and the crickets chirping, but he was ready to press the button when needed.

He slept soundly that night and didn't wake up at all throughout the night. He had good dreams. They were dreams of pressing the nut-button anytime there was too much noise. He dreamed everyone found out about his invention and wanted it as well and Hat Squirrel hired him to install soundproofing in everyone's home.

When he woke up, he wasn't awakened by the sound of a trumpet. This was surprising, since every day Gary woke him up that way. He could hear the birds chirping, singing their beautiful morning songs. He could hear the sounds of some Squirrels out for a morning scurry along the paths. He could feel the sun shining gently on his face through the window. He could smell the calm, nice smell of rotting leaves.

As he lay there, he thought about the smell. He didn't normally like the smell of rotting leaves. In fact, he realized he still didn't like that smell. He also wasn't sure why he would be smelling that smell.

He continued to lay there with the sun shining on his face as he thought this one through. The only time he smelled that smell around his home was when Gary was around. He was sure, however, that Gary couldn't be outside his window. For one thing, Gary was big. If Gary was outside the window, Jerry was sure there would be no sunlight shining through the open window because Gary would block all the light.

The other reason was that the smell was far too strong. It wasn't like Gary was outside the window, it was like Gary was right next to Jerry!

Jerry opened his eyes and looked straight into the smiling face of Gary.

"Ahhh!" Jerry screamed. "What are you doing in my house and why are you staring at me while I'm sleeping? What's going on?"

"I didn't want to wake you up with the loud sound of the trumpet, so I'm coming in close to you to play it quietly," Gary explained. He then raised the trumpet up to his lips and quietly blew the one note from the one song he played. He blew it gently, then blew it again, then again.

Jerry was leaning back against the wall with a frown on his face. This was far worse than the trumpet playing outside his house.

He was just about to explain this to Gary when his elbow hit the nut-button. Instantly the window covering slammed down just above Jerry's head, and he could hear the ones over the window and door in the other room slam down as well. They were sealed in and soundproofed from the rest of the world.

"What just happened?" Gary screamed!

"Oh, it's nothing. It's just my soundproofing. I just press this button right here and…" Jerry started to explain.

Unfortunately, he was interrupted by Gary's growl. As soon as he saw the nut shaped button, he had started to drool uncontrollably and then quickly growled as he lunged for it with his teeth. In one simple bite, the button was gone.

"No, you can't eat that!" Jerry hollered.

"Um, I'm sorry. I eat when I get scared. This whole sound proofing thing you have scared me a lot. You know, though, that nut was kind of stale. It didn't taste very good," Gary said.

Jerry frowned again. "It was made out of wood. It shouldn't taste good. It was also the way that we open up the windows and doors. Now I have to figure out a way to get us out of here."

"What? You mean we could be stuck in here forever?" Gary said, looking very nervous.

"No, I'll find a way to open the doors. They are made of solid wood so it won't be easy to chew through them. I'll have to find a way to make a new button or something," Jerry said as he shook his head.

"I don't like the idea of being stuck in here. It makes me nervous. Jerry?"

"Yes, Gary?"

"I sweat when I'm nervous."

"Okay. Thank you for telling me that, Gary."

"No, Jerry, I don't think you understand. I sweat badly when I'm nervous. And mom tells me that my sweat does not smell very nice."

"What? How bad can it be? It can't be... Whoa!!" Jerry yelled. He fell backward and rolled right off his bed, landing on the floor next to Gary. That put him closer to Gary who, by this point, was sweating so bad he was dripping.

He had never smelled anything quite like it. It was kind of like the smell of rotting leaves, times one hundred. Plus, there was the smell of stinky feet, old cheese and rotten eggs... also times one hundred. On top of this, it was only getting worse the more Gary sweat. On top of even that, Jerry began to realize that the house was not only soundproof, but it was also now smell proof. That meant the smell couldn't get out, it just all stayed inside the house.

"I have to calm myself down," Gary said. "I have to find a way to stop being nervous, so I don't sweat anymore. What can I do to calm myself down?" Gary started moving around Jerry's house as if he were looking for something to do to get his mind off of the fact that they were now sealed in a sound proof house. Finally, his eyes landed on the trumpet.

"I'll play the trumpet," he yelled and lunged for the instrument. He grabbed it quickly, and before Jerry could stop him, he started to play his two-note song over and over again. The more he played, the louder it was.

Jerry hollered at him to stop, but Gary couldn't hear him over the sound of the trumpet playing. Jerry then started to wave his arms and jump around, but Gary seemed to think that Jerry was dancing to the sound of the trumpet and smiled as he played even faster, louder and in a way that involved much more spit coming out the end. The more Jerry jumped around, the more Gary played with enthusiasm.

Jerry realized the only way to stop the madness was to fix the button and fix it fast. He ran to his desk and desperately tried to think of a way to build a new button out of the supplies he had. He had used most of his supplies, and the only ones he had left were in his shed. The shed was outside the house. Outside the house was where it was quiet and not smelly.

Finally, he found a nut in the kitchen and ran in to attach it to the button. He secured it perfectly and was about to press the nut button to release the windows when the playing stopped, and Gary reached out with his mouth and chomped down on the nut button, chewing it up and swallowing it.

"No!" Jerry hollered, now able to be heard. "We needed that for the…" but Gary couldn't hear him. He had started playing again, but this time chunks of nuts were flying out the end of the trumpet with the spit. It didn't make it nicer.

He tried again with another nut from the kitchen, but Gary really could move fast to eat nuts when he was nervous. Jerry realized he had to find another way.

Four hours later, Jerry had managed to find an old invention in the back of his closet. He took it apart to see what he could use. In the end, he used the handle from the invention and attached it to the button. Gary tried to take a bite of it, but it was too hard.

Jerry pressed the new button, and the door and windows swung open. As they opened, there was a hissing sound as the smell escaped.

Both Squirrels ran outside to get some fresh air, only to find the Squirrels around Erry-Ville all gasping and choking because the smell from Jerry's house had just escaped.

Once the smell had cleared out a bit, Jerry took apart his soundproofing invention. He realized it wasn't worth it in case Gary decided to do something special to wake him up again. He had to find another way to wake up peacefully.

Nut Beetles Part I

Jerry was a Squirrel. Jerry was also an inventor... quite a good one, as a matter of fact. He could design and build just about anything. The problem was, Jerry's inventions rarely worked the way he wanted them to work.

Jerry woke up to the normal sound of a trumpet playing. Gary played the trumpet every morning. It was nice in one sense because Gary was trying to play it for Jerry. It was like Gary was giving Jerry a gift.

Unfortunately, Gary was not a good trumpet player. In fact, he was a terrible one. He only seemed to know three songs. The first one was a song with one note, played over and over again. The second song had two notes. Gary played these two notes over and over again. The third song had no notes and many notes. It was just Gary blowing on the trumpet. Whatever came out was his song.

All three songs were torture for Jerry to listen to.

This morning's song was the third kind. There were notes and squeaks with the occasional gurgle sound followed by a loud splash as Gary's drool built up inside the trumpet and then escaped. It was pretty gross.

The trumpet playing usually went on for quite a while, but this time it only lasted about an hour. When Gary had finally finished, Jerry took the time to calm himself down and wipe away some tears. He then stood up and moved to the kitchen. He found himself a nice breakfast of nuts and drank some water before heading outside for a late summer morning stroll.

It was a beautiful day and, now that Gary was finished with his blow and splash approach to the trumpet, Jerry could enjoy himself. He wandered about, smelling the fresh summer air and feeling at peace.

As he strolled down the path, a new sound caught his ear. It was a sound he had not heard quite like this for many years. It was a loud, buzzing sound.

In truth, he heard that sound every single year about this time. In late summer, the Nut Beetles would come. They were mostly harmless. They would burrow into the nuts and eat them, but since there were normally only a few here and there, no one really minded. No one noticed when they arrived because they were so quiet, but you could hear them buzzing around when you collected nuts at harvest time.

Unfortunately, every now and then, the Nut Beetles would come in the thousands. You could hear them arrive because thousands of Nut Beetles flying in a swarm made a huge amount of noise.

The noise of the Nut Beetles, however, was not the problem. A few Nut Beetles would eat a few nuts. Thousands of Nut Beetles could eat all the nuts. If they ate all the nuts, the Squirrels would starve.

Jerry ran straight for the village center. It was located on the far side of the village, a little ways outside of town. Jerry had suggested many times that they change the name to something like, "village outside," but no one thought it was a good idea.

As he ran, he could see all the other Squirrels making their way to the village center as well. Everyone knew this was an emergency.

He arrived to find that most of the village Squirrels were already there. Everyone was in a panic. There was screaming and yelling and crying everywhere Jerry looked.

As soon as Hat Squirrel arrived, he jumped up on the center speaking rock which was on the north side of the village center which was a little ways outside of town. The speaking rock was for speaking, and once Hat Squirrel stood on the rock, no one was allowed to speak without his permission.

A hush fell over the crowd, and Hat Squirrel opened his mouth. Jerry thought for sure he would tell them what to do, but instead, he looked at each of them and screamed. His face scrunched up, and he screamed again. This continued for far too long. This was clearly too much for Hat Squirrel.

When Hat Squirrel had calmed down a little bit, he spoke to the crowd in a shaky voice. "They have arrived. The Nut Beetles. They will eat all our nuts, and we will starve. It is all over. There is nothing that can be done."

With that, Hat Squirrel collapsed and rolled off the speaking rock. All the assembled Squirrels fell down as well and cried.

Hat Squirrel was off the rock so Jerry could speak up. "Wait! What if we do what we did last time this happened?"

Mary stood up and gave Jerry a scolding look. "Okay, wise guy. Tell us, what did we do last time this happened?"

"We went to the Beetle Birds and asked them for help. They came and ate most of the Nut Beetles and chased the rest away," Jerry said. He didn't know why no one else remembered. "If we leave now and travel fast, we can get to them before the nut harvest is lost."

Squirrels around the village center began to nod their heads as if they were remembering, but Jerry was pretty sure they weren't. They were just hoping someone would solve the problem for them.

Hat Squirrel pulled himself together and climbed up on the rock again. The crowd grew silent again and waited for their leader to speak.

"I have had an idea," Hat Squirrel began.

Jerry rolled his eyes. He knew where this was going.

"I can save us. I have a way to end this plague that has fallen upon us. We must turn to the Beetle Birds for help. Do we have any questions?"

"I don't have a question," Larry said. "I just want to say that I think you are so wise, Hat Squirrel. No one else could have come up with such a wonderful solution."

"Yes, it is true," Hat Squirrel agreed. "I am very wise. Much wiser than anyone else here, especially Jerry." With that, he looked over at Jerry and nodded to him. "You may approach the rock, young Squirrel."

Jerry was pretty sure he was older than Hat Squirrel. "Yes, Hat Squirrel. How may I help you?"

"You, young Squirrel, are to be our ambassador to go to the Beetle Birds. You must go with all haste and bring them here. It must be you as there are only two Squirrels in existence who know the way to the Beetle Birds. I, of course, am one of them, but no one can ask me to tell them the way because I won't tell them. You, Jerry, are the other Squirrel who knows the way, so you must go. Time is of the essence. There is no time to delay. You must go immediately. This very moment. You do not even have time for me to finish this sentence. Why have you not gone, yet?" Hat Squirrel looked annoyed.

Jerry found himself rolling his eyes again. "Okay, I'll go. I'm heading out now." The journey to the Beetle Birds would only take about a day, that is if he could keep his speed up the whole way. He was a Squirrel so he could move pretty fast when he needed to.

As he was about to run off to the southeast, in the direction of the Beetle Birds, he heard a voice. It was Sherry, the old lady Squirrel who lived in his upstairs apartment. She was Gary's mom. She slowly made her way toward the rock, using her cane to walk.

"I'm so sorry to speak without permission, Hat Squirrel. May I make a request?" she said in her sweet voice. She was carrying a plate of cookies and handed them to Hat Squirrel.

Hat Squirrel took the cookies. Jerry was about to warn Hat Squirrel about how she made them warm but decided to hold his tongue. Hat Squirrel gobbled them up. "Ooooh! They're still warm!"

Jerry had to look away. He found that kind of thing to be pretty gross.

Hat Squirrel nodded to Sherry to give her permission to speak, and she made her request. "Hat Squirrel, dear, you are such a lovely young man. I am so impressed with your hat wearing."

It never hurt to compliment Hat Squirrel. He always appreciated it and smiled back warmly.

"I would like to go with young Jerry. Would it be okay, dear, if I joined him as he travels to the Beetle Birds?" She smiled sweetly again.

Jerry turned to leave. He knew he didn't have much time and there was no way Hat Squirrel would let her come. She was far too slow with that cane, and Jerry could move much faster by himself.

Hat Squirrel, however, was quite taken by her sweetness, her cookies and her compliments. "Ms. Sherry, of course you can join him." He then looked in Jerry's direction. "Jerry! Jerry! Ms. Sherry will be joining you!"

"Thanks, dear," she said to Hat Squirrel before turning to Jerry. "Jerry, dear, will you give me a hand with my knitting? I'll want to bring it with me for when we stop for breaks and for meals and for snacks and for nighttime and for rests and for naps and for looking at the beautiful scenery. Oh, and I would like to buy some cookies and warm them up for the trip."

"We don't have time for this..." Jerry began to say but was cut off by Hat Squirrel.

"Silence! Ms. Sherry will be joining you! Hat Squirrel has spoken. It has been decided." With that, he jumped down off the rock, and everyone left. They appeared happy. It was as if they thought the problem of the Nut Beetles had been solved.

Jerry knew at the speed Sherry traveled, they wouldn't get to the Beetle Birds until sometime after the end of harvest time. The nuts would be eaten, and all would be lost.

He had an idea. A good idea.

He ran back to his house and to his desk. It was time to invent.

He set out to make up the plans for the invention and then set to work on building it. He normally had all the parts he needed somewhere in his house as he regularly collected anything he saw that looked useful. He put it all together and smiled to himself. This could solve the problem.

He ran outside in time to see Sherry hobbling down the last few steps from the upstairs apartment. She slowly made her way over to him. Gary came down behind her. He was huge. He was also carrying a large pack.

"Jerry, dear, would you be so kind as to carry my luggage? Gary has it," she said as she smiled sweetly.

She really was a nice lady. She just didn't seem to notice that they needed to rush.

"Um, sure. I can carry that. But before I do, I want to show you my invention. Can I see your cane?" Jerry stretched out his hand so she could hand him the cane and he could install his invention.

"Of course, dear." She handed him her cane and then immediately fell over.

She hit the ground pretty hard but smiled sweetly up at him with a look of pain on her face. Jerry felt really bad. He had not expected her to just fall down like that.

He set to work on installing his invention. It didn't take long. When he was done, he handed it back to Sherry.

"Thank you, dear. It's nice to not fall over." She stood up and looked at the end of the cane. "What is it, dear?"

"It's a wheel attachment for your cane. Instead of having to walk at a slow speed, you can drive the cane really fast!" He pointed out the little spots for her feet and showed her how to power it so she could move forward.

When it appeared as though she understood everything, he turned toward her luggage. He grabbed her pack and threw it up over his shoulders. It was far heavier than he would have thought. He wondered how many cookies she had packed! At least with the powered cane, they could move at a faster speed.

He turned back to Sherry to tell her it was time to go only to see her lying on the ground again. Her cane was underneath Gary. He was trying to drive it himself. The invention was not meant to carry such weight, and Jerry yelled for him to get off of it, but he was too late. The cane began to smoke and putter and then ground to a halt.

"No! We needed that to be able to get to the Beetle Birds quickly!" Jerry yelled. Gary was nice, but he had just ruined the very thing that would help them save the nut harvest.

"It's okay, dear," Sherry said from her position on the ground. "We'll be okay."

Gary handed her the cane, and she hopped up on it. It still moved with her tiny size, but just barely faster than she would have walked. Jerry lumbered after her as they made their way toward the Beetle Birds.

This was going to be a long trip. Jerry feared they would not make it to the Beetle Birds in time…

To be continued…

10

Nut Beetles Part II

After about five hours, they stopped for supper. Jerry looked back with frustration and stared at the village. The village was only about a two-minute run from where they were stopped. Two minutes, that was, if Jerry had been able to travel on his own.

Sherry pulled out a plate of cookies. They looked quite tasty, and Jerry was about to grab one and bite into it, but she pulled them away.

"No, my dear, cookies should be warm when they are eaten. They always taste better that way." With that, she sat on the plate.

Jerry spent a few minutes trying to convince her he preferred un-sat-upon cookies, but she would not hear of it. She insisted this was the only way to eat cookies.

Ten minutes later, as Jerry munched on the last of the butt-warmed snacks, he thought about the journey ahead. He wondered how he could manage to get to the Beetle Birds and save the harvest when they were moving at such a slow speed.

When they settled down for the night, Jerry found that Sherry wanted to tuck him in. He didn't mind at first as the thought made him think back to his mom when he was a little Squirrel. She covered him up with a warm blanket. He tried not to think about how she had warmed the blanket. She then leaned in and gave him a goodnight kiss on the forehead.

Jerry was shocked to find that she drooled terribly. After such a little kiss on his forehead, he felt like his entire head was wet. He could feel the drool slide down into his ear. It wasn't a nice feeling.

She smiled down at him and said, "Goodnight, dear. Don't let the Nut Beetles bite."

The next morning, Jerry awoke to find Sherry at work on the invention. She looked like she was fixing it.

"I didn't know you knew how to do that kind of thing," Jerry said.

"Oh, I learned how to fix broken inventions when I was working as a mercenary for the Mudmen king way back before you were born, dear," Sherry explained.

"A mercenary?" Jerry asked, a little shocked.

"Never mind that, dear. I know you don't really know how to build things all that well. You try, but obviously, from how slow this drives, you must not know how to build a proper super-scooter. I figured I'd better help you out."

Jerry grumbled to himself. "It worked fine until Gary sat on it."

"Yes, dear, I'm sure it did. You keep telling yourself that, but in the meantime, I will make it work properly."

She worked for a few more minutes and then closed it up again. "That should just about do it. Let's get going, dear."

Jerry quickly packed up. When he was ready, she started up the super-scooter.

Unfortunately, Jerry blinked at the moment of take-off. Because he blinked, he lost sight of her almost immediately. When his eyes focused again after her take-off, there was nothing but a trail of smoke off into the distance. It took him a moment or two before he realized she was gone. She had not just fixed the super-scooter, she had super-charged it!

He raced off in the direction he was sure she had gone, but could only find a deep rut in the ground where she had been driving. In a few moments, he began to see signs of her travel. There were bushes knocked down flat, tracks going through the dirt in other spots and even a small tree had been entirely ripped out by the roots and tossed to the side. At one point there was a tree that Jerry figured she must have hit straight on. Right in the middle of the trunk of the tree, there was a shape of an old-lady-Squirrel riding a super-scooter cane. The old-lady-Squirrel shape was drilled right through the center of the tree. From the way the hole in the trunk of the tree showed her arms sticking out and her head off to the side with her mouth open, Jerry figured she must be terrified.

He knew he had to catch up quickly. He rushed after her and after a few minutes, he saw her. She was screaming wildly and driving straight up the trunk of a large oak tree.

He raced to the bottom of the tree, but by this point, she was driving down a large tree branch. When she reached the end of the branch, she jumped through the air from that branch to a branch on another tree.

He ran over to the other tree and climbed up the trunk. His heart was beating wildly as he thought about how scared she must be… that was, until he managed to get close to her. He could hear her screams, but they were screams of joy. She was having fun!

"Whhhheeeeeeee!!!!!" Sherry screamed. "Jerry! This is the most fun I've had since I fought against the Chimpanzee army back when I was just a young Squirrel like you! I just about have control of this cane… just another second…" With that, Sherry managed to turn the cane and drive down the side of a trunk. She came to a stop at the bottom.

When Jerry found her at the foot of the tree, she had a big smile on her face and looked pleased with herself. "Grab hold, Jerry!"

"What? Grab hold?" Jerry asked, quite confused.

"Grab hold! We have some Beetle Birds to find!"

Jerry came up behind her and reached for the cane. As soon as his hand wrapped around it, Sherry took off again with a scream of joy.

They moved so fast, Jerry's entire body stretched out behind the cane. He had to grip the cane like his life depended on it. Jerry wondered if it really did.

At the speeds at which they were traveling, it didn't take long to reach Beetle Bird Territory. Jerry called up to her, "We need to stop and talk to them. The Beetle Birds can be really grumpy. We have to be very polite."

"No time!" Sherry hollered back as they continued to race along. "We have to move. The Nut Beetles are doing a lot of damage. There's no time for chit-chat."

"But if we don't talk to them, how are we going to get them to go back with us?" Jerry hollered as they continued to drive.

"This is how!" Sherry yelled back.

She turned the super-scooter toward a large tree. Jerry looked up and could see a huge number of Beetle Birds resting in the tree above, but watching the two of them warily.

When they came to the bottom of the tree, Sherry drove the cane directly up the side of the tree, dragging poor Jerry behind her. He could see the birds were starting to look a little nervous, and some were starting to look angry.

This, however, did not stop Sherry. She made for a large group of birds on one of the large branches, closer to the ground and drove straight into the middle of them.

Before Jerry could do anything to stop her, she ran right into one of the birds.

Feathers flew in every direction, and Jerry looked back to see the bird she had hit. It had a bare stretch of skin showing along its back where the feathers had been ripped off. The Beetle Bird did not look happy. The rest of the Beetle Birds did not look happy either. Jerry looked up at Sherry. Sherry turned and looked down at Jerry. Sherry did look happy.

"I think it's going to work!" she shouted above the wind and the growing sound of angry birds behind them.

"What have you done? What's going to work?" Jerry yelled back.

"Watch and see!" she replied.

Sherry then drove the cane off the end of the branch and landed down on the ground, still traveling at breakneck speeds. She turned the cane around, so they were traveling back in the direction of Erry-Ville.

Jerry looked over his shoulder in fear. The entire flock of Beetle Birds, maybe hundreds, maybe thousands, were flying up into the sky and turning down toward Jerry and Sherry.

"They're coming after us!" screamed Jerry.

"Perfect," Sherry replied. "It did work!"

With that, she yelled out a "yeeeehaaww" and drove off away from the birds.

Jerry looked back and immediately wished he had not. The birds were just about to grab him, but at the last second, Sherry turned a little to the left, then to the right, then back to the left again to evade the birds.

"We'll have to be quick to get away," Sherry explained as they drove down the path back toward Erry-Ville. "If not, they'll get us both and eat us. This was such a good idea!"

"What about this seems like a good idea to you, Sherry?" Jerry yelled as he continued to hold on with his hands while his legs and body trailed behind the cane.

"No time for chit-chat, Jerry. We have some birds to avoid! I think the best thing to do is to drive through that thorn patch up ahead. That'll slow the birds down!"

"Thorns? No! Wait, Sherry! Let's talk this through," Jerry said in a panic.

"No time for thinking! We must act," Sherry yelled back as she drove straight into the thorns.

Jerry thought to himself that Sherry was somehow managing to hit each and every thorn imaginable in that patch. He found himself saying, "Ouch" so many times he finally grew bored with it and just took each thorn in turn. When they drove out the other side, Jerry noticed that Sherry did not have a single thorn stuck in her, but he could barely see his own fur through all the thorns stuck in his side.

The trip back to Erry-Ville continued like this the rest of way. The birds continued to chase them and every time they grew close, Sherry would drive into another thorn patch to slow the birds down. Jerry didn't think the thorns were actually slowing the birds down, but they sure hurt.

After about what felt like a week, but was probably only a few minutes, Jerry could see Erry-Ville up ahead. It wasn't much farther, but the birds were still right on his tail. If he and Sherry weren't quick, they wouldn't make it.

He looked up into the trees and, sure enough, the Nut Beetles were all still there. They had eaten a lot of the nuts, but there would still be enough left if the Beetle Birds drove the Nut Beetles away.

"Flerry!" Jerry yelled. He had trouble speaking since he had about eighteen thorns stuck in his lips and tongue. "Wha' ahhh you gow-ing chtoo thdo thnow?"

"Now that the Beetle Birds are angry, I think we should introduce them to the Nut Beetles, don't you think?" Sherry yelled back to Jerry.

"Thure," Jerry said through the thorns.

Sherry then drove the cane right into the middle of Erry-Ville. Squirrels dove for cover, trying to protect themselves from the crazy cane driver. Sherry drove the cane up the side of one of the largest nut-producing trees in Erry-Ville.

Jerry could hear the sound of the Nut Beetles, buzzing away. None of them seemed to notice what was happening, but as Sherry arrived at the top, she drove right into the middle of a swarm of Nut Beetles.

The Beetles scattered every which way. At first, they were only trying to avoid Sherry and Jerry, but then the birds arrived.

The Nut Beetles were surprised. They were suddenly faced with their greatest enemy—the Beetle Birds. The Beetle Birds were surprised because they had not realized until that moment that it was lunchtime.

The Beetle Birds went right for the Nut Beetles and immediately started to eat them all up. The Nut Beetles scattered every which way they could.

Sherry drove the cane down the side of the tree and came to a stop. She looked around with a big smile on her face.

Jerry let go of the super-scooter and rolled on the ground. The thorns were stuck in everywhere. There were so many, he really was just an unrecognizable ball of thorns. He did not enjoy the experience.

"Sherry!" Hat Squirrel called out. "Welcome back! I see you have saved the day. I'm so glad you saved us, and I'm kind of glad that you lost Jerry along the way. He's always causing so much trouble."

"No, he's right inside that ball of thorns right there," Sherry explained.

"Oh," Hat Squirrel said, looking at the ball of thorns and trying to see if he could spot Jerry inside. "Well, you can't have everything. Thanks again for saving the town. I would give you a medal or something, but I just don't want to. Bye!"

With that, Hat Squirrel walked away. All the Squirrels quickly smiled at Sherry and then went back to what they were doing before the Nut Beetles showed up. Sherry reached down, pulled Jerry's invention off the bottom of her cane and slowly began to make her way back to her apartment.

"Help," Jerry whimpered. "Is anyone there? Oh no, help!" he cried out as he started to roll away down the hill in his thorn ball.

You can find more Jerry stories in Jerry the Squirrel: Volume Two!

* * *

If you like Jerry the Squirrel, consider leaving reviews for this book on Amazon, Goodreads, BAM, Chapters and more! These reviews help more than you might realize… and they make Shawn feel good.

Chapter One from Arestana Book I
The Key Quest

Arestana: The Key Quest
(Sneak Peek)

Liam ran for his life. If he couldn't keep ahead of the footsteps behind him, he wasn't sure he would live to see tomorrow. Harry was mad. Really mad.

Liam continued to run. Not only was Harry mad, but he was also fast. There wasn't a kid at school who could outrun him once he was at full speed. He could move! Harry's weakness, however, was his start. Harry would always start out slow. He would take a few steps and then begin to gain speed. Each step would carry him faster and faster. Once he was at full speed, there was no way to stop him.

The only hope anyone had was to change direction. Each time someone turned, Harry would have to take the time to pick up speed again.

Liam heard the pound of Harry's feet close behind him and turned sharply to his left down a side street. He heard

Harry fly past him. The big guy had narrowly missed his target. It would take Harry a moment to bring himself to a stop and then figure out where Liam had gone. Then Harry would need some time to pick up speed again.

Liam wasn't far from home. He had run all the way from school, and he was exhausted. He never got used to those daily chases. If he could only make it home, he would be safe. Harry seemed to have a great deal of trouble figuring out which house was Liam's. They lived right next door to each other, but Harry wasn't the brightest guy in the world. Once Liam was out of sight, Harry struggled to remember where Liam lived. He had to get home.

Liam pushed his legs a little harder. He thought he could make it when he heard Harry's footsteps approach again from behind. He must have managed to turn around quickly and start running after Liam again.

Liam turned sharply down a side path. He couldn't remember where that path went but assumed it would come out somewhere, and he'd be able to find his way home from there.

As he ran down the path, something odd happened. He felt a strong pull. He wasn't sure what it was, but it made him feel as though he needed to go somewhere. He pushed the thought out of his mind. Now wasn't the time. He had more important things to worry about.

Harry came upon the path Liam had turned down, but he didn't quite make the turn. Liam heard him slam into the fence which lined the side of the path. Liam smiled to himself, but he knew he would pay for that one. He was sure of it.

The path continued past the two houses and opened up to a little park. It was a nice park. The grass was well cared for. There were swings, a slide and some climbing equipment. It was also safe for children to play there in the sense that a fence surrounded the entire park. The only way in or out was the path he had just come through.

This was not good for Liam.

Liam came to a stop and scanned the outer rim of the park again just to make sure. There was no way out. The wooden fence around the outside was tall. Liam might be able to climb it, but it would slow him down enough that Harry would be able to catch him.

Liam heard the footsteps behind him come to a stop. He turned around, and Harry stood in the entrance, blocking the only way in or out of the park. He walked up close enough for Liam to smell him. Harry normally smelled of onions or garlic. Today was garlic.

Harry stared at him for a moment. Liam had always been one of Harry's favorite targets.

The bully stepped close and stood only a step or two away. He was about four inches taller than Liam and roughly forty pounds heavier. After that run, he didn't even seem to be breathing heavy. Harry was a tank!

He bared his teeth and spoke up, "Hello, Ed."

The first few months after Liam had met Harry, he had thought Harry was somehow trying to make fun of him by calling him "Ed." Liam didn't know what was funny about the name "Ed," but assumed Harry meant it to be mean. In time, however, Liam came to believe Harry honestly thought Liam's name was "Ed." No amount of evidence seemed to convince Harry it could be anything else. From the first day they'd met, six years ago, when Liam had moved into his house and bumped into his next-door neighbor Harry, he had consistently called Liam, "Ed."

"Hello, Harry. Nice day for a run."

Harry growled. He looked at Liam as though he needed a moment to figure out how best to torture him.

Liam started to feel the same pull he had felt earlier. This time it felt like his whole body was being sucked somewhere. He put out a foot in the direction of the pull to steady himself and focused back on Harry. Whatever it was, he had more important things to deal with at the moment.

Liam had tried to stand up to Harry many times over the years. He had tried to fight back, but Harry was too strong. He had tried to outrun him, but Harry was too fast. Sometimes he found he could talk his way out of the situation. That was his plan this time. He had prepared something new for today.

Liam had learned the key to talking his way out of an encounter with Harry was to confuse him. If Harry could make sense of everything, he would get bored and turn back to his favorite activity: torturing Liam. If Liam could confuse him just a little bit, he might be able to get away.

"Did you hear about Liam?" Liam asked. There were few things Harry liked more than picking on other kids, but one of them was gossip.

Harry's face lit up with excitement. He grabbed Liam by the shoulders and pulled him in close. Their noses almost touched as he yelled, "Tell me, Ed!"

The best way to confuse Harry was to talk about someone Harry didn't think existed. The perfect person to talk about, then, was Liam. Harry didn't appear to know a Liam, only an "Ed."

"Liam broke his leg."

Harry looked upset. Liam suspected it wasn't out of concern for this "Liam," but because Harry hadn't been involved.

"How did he break his leg?"

"He fell up his basement stairs at home."

Liam gave Harry a moment or two to absorb his answer. He could see confusion in Harry's eyes as the larger boy tried to make sense of it all. Liam felt things were going well.

"He fell... up... the stairs?"

"Yah! Of course, not just one flight. That would be silly. He fell up from the basement, rolled all the way into the kitchen, down the hallway and up to the second floor. The poor guy looks terrible. He's covered in bruises. The doctors think he won't walk again for thousands of minutes."

Liam had prepared all that a few days before. He hoped it would confuse Harry long enough to give him a chance to get away.

Harry looked upset again. His face dropped, and he looked down at the ground. Liam was pretty sure he saw a tear form in one of Harry's eyes. He didn't know what to do.

"Uh, Harry?"

"Yah, Ed?"

"You okay?"

"Well, I'm just kinda sad, you know? I had planned to meet up with Liam later on today. I was going to maybe beat him up or something."

Liam was now confused. "You were going to meet up with him?"

"Yah, I had him in my schedule." He pulled out a little book and showed Liam his weekly planner. He noticed "Ed" was written on each page. Sure enough, later that day, Harry had the name "Leeum" written in for the evening with the words, "beet upp" scribbled underneath.

Liam started to suspect things were about to turn out poorly for him. It was easier to talk about someone Harry didn't seem to know. Who was the other Liam?

He had forgotten all about the pull when it ramped up again. Liam thought he could feel himself slide a little bit on the ground. Things were getting weird.

Harry growled again, and it brought Liam's thoughts back to the danger he faced. Harry's jaw tightened, and he looked at Liam like he was mad. "Ed! You tell Liam I want to meet him right here at lunchtime today. I don't care if he has a broken leg. He will meet me here or else!"

Things were starting to turn out poorly. Harry didn't take kindly to people who didn't do what he told them. Liam didn't know if there even was another Liam. He certainly couldn't bring him here. Even if he could find another Liam willing to come, that other Liam probably didn't have a broken leg, and then the real Liam would have to explain that one. On top of it all, Harry wanted the "Liam" kid there at lunchtime. It was already about four in the afternoon. There was no way Liam could survive the whole thing.

Liam looked down to see his feet start to slide. The invisible force was dragging him toward the side of the park! He tried to plant his feet firmly on the ground and leaned off to the side away from the pull.

Harry didn't seem to notice anything out of the ordinary at first. He continued, "If you don't get him here in time, Ed, I'll fight you instead. Uh, Ed, what are you doing?"

Liam looked down. He was at a perfect forty-five-degree angle. He knew enough about gravity to know that he should fall right about then. Whatever was pulling him was strong.

Harry looked worried. He walked around beside Liam and stared at him on an angle. Harry was not good at things like angles or gravity or intelligent thought, but he knew enough to see that something wasn't quite right.

Liam reached down and grabbed hold of a clump of grass on the ground to try to keep himself in place. The pull grew stronger. He started to slip, and Harry laughed as he watched Liam dragged by some unseen force over the grass of the park and toward one of the fences.

Liam hit the fence and came to a stop. The force which had taken hold of him couldn't seem to pull him through the fence. Liam was happy about that.

"Harry, something weird is happening. Go get help!"

Harry looked at Liam for a moment before shaking his head. "No, Ed. I think this is for the best."

"What? What are you talking about? What's for the best? I've been pulled into a fence by an invisible force!"

"Whatever is holding you there is going to help me." Harry smiled and charged at Liam.

127

Liam yelled. This was going to hurt. Harry ran as fast as he could toward him. He quickly closed the gap between them, and Liam couldn't budge from his position.

Just as Harry was about to hit him, Liam felt the pull grow stronger, and he slid up the fence and over the top. He heard the crash where Harry had hit the boards, but he had more important things on his mind. He hit the ground and slid through someone's backyard. He then slid between two houses and out toward the street. Once out front, the force pulling his body turned him, and he slid down the sidewalk. He could see he wasn't far from home.

He rounded a corner and saw his house up ahead. Some of his neighbors were outside. He hollered for help, but most just took pictures with their phones and yelled that that was the coolest thing they had ever seen.

He slid across the front lawn of his house and up the front steps. He slammed against the front door. Whatever pulled him wanted him in the house. He reached for the handle and slowly turned it. The door flew open, and he tumbled in. The force pulled him down the hallway and into the kitchen.

His parents were both in the kitchen as usual, hard at work baking. Today Liam smelled chocolate chip cookies. There were what looked like fifty dozen cookies all piled up on the counter.

Liam grabbed the counter and held on for dear life. He looked over to see his parents staring at him with a look of curiosity on their faces. He realized it must have been quite the sight. He held onto the counter with both hands, his body and legs extended straight out about three feet above the floor.

His dad spoke up first, "Hmm... that's unusual. You don't normally suspend yourself above the floor like that, Liam, do you?"

"No, Dad, this is new for me," Liam replied.

"How was school, dear?" Liam's mom asked.

Liam couldn't believe how relaxed they appeared to be about the whole, "Liam floating above the ground, held up by nothing but his two hands gripping the counter" thing. He would have thought they would find it all a little more unnerving.

"Help me! I'm being dragged somewhere by some unseen force!"

"That's nice, Liam. Glad school went well today," his mom responded before both parents turned back to the cookies. Liam lost his grip on the counter and continued through the kitchen. On his way, he managed to grab a handful of cookies. He didn't know where he would end up but thought he would need to keep up his energy.

The pull dragged him up the stairs and around the corner. He slid down the hallway and grabbed the doorframe of his bedroom. He held on for a moment and peered inside the room. He was instantly hit by the smell of dirty clothes and poor ventilation. The room looked like someone had gone through everything he owned, dumped out his drawers and tossed everything around. He was comforted to know at least his room was the same as always.

He lost his grip and slid farther down the hallway toward the bathroom. The door was open, and he could see the toilet straight ahead. As he was dragged closer, he looked in horror as the toilet seat slowly raised. Somehow, he knew the pull was dragging him toward the toilet. He cried out in fear. He didn't know what was going on, but he knew he did not want to be flushed. He wondered if he could even fit down the toilet drain. He suddenly had an image flash in his mind of a plumber explaining to his parents that there was a thirteen-year-old boy clogging their toilet drain.

As he entered the bathroom, he grabbed for the doorframe. The whole room turned into a windstorm, and he could see that inside the toilet was a swirl of colors. Liam began to scream for help. He hoped someone could hear him above the wind.

The wind grabbed his feet. It pulled one foot into the toilet. Liam imagined his obituary: "Liam, died thirteen years old, sucked into a toilet. Death by flushing. A fitting end for such a young life."

By that time, both feet were well into the toilet. He called again for help, but no one seemed to hear. His fingers held on as long as they could, but his grip began to weaken. With one last yell, Liam went in. His whole body disappeared down the drain.

Liam had been flushed.

Continued in Arestana Book I: The Key Quest

*　　*　　*

If you like the Arestana Series, consider leaving reviews for this book on Amazon, Goodreads, BAM, Chapters and more! These reviews help more than you might realize… and they make Shawn feel good.

Check out these books by

Shawn P. B. Robinson

Jerry the Squirrel: Volume I

Jerry the Squirrel: Volume II

Jerry the Squirrel: Volume III (coming 2019)

Arestana I: The Key Quest

Arestana II: The Defense Quest

Arestana III: The Harry Quest

#bewarethechicken